God of

by Bee R

Hello! I'm Bee Rosen!

I am an English author who started writing stories as soon as I had learned to use a pen. A natural and mystical theme travelled throughout them all. But over the course of almost a decade, I became visually impaired and lost the ability to write stories. Now, at 23, I have written my first book since. With the help of assistive technology and new strategies to manage my now stabilised sight loss, I introduce to you 'God of Alba'.

CHAPTER 1:

Smoke before Emrun

The sun beat down on the land of Alba, in the city of 'Emrun'. Every Viking hut shone and looked as if it was kindling for a greater heat. Three brothers returned from battle victorious. Dub, Dother and Dain were mighty men with Viking fires for hair. They stood taller than almost anyone and they almost always brought destruction as a group. Feared in every corner of the kingdom of Alba, they behaved exactly as they wished according to every emotional whim. The land of Alba was the oldest and most beautiful kingdom of all known realms. Mountains of greys and greens, valleys of heather, bright skies and animals of majesty.

Across the glen came Dain, the eldest brother of the

three, who started calling for their youngest sister Kenina. A red headed girl, with a spirit of fire. She was not by any means tall in stature or even strong, but her mind had adapted to survive the perilous brothers of her kin.

"Kenina! Come and see us! Bring us drinks! We the victorious!" came the shouts of Dain.

The brothers entered their hut to see drinks perfectly laid out and everything their foolish drunkard minds had requested. But Kenina was nowhere to be seen. Seemingly having preempted their intoxication, she had disappeared. Their mother Lilith, stood quietly in the hut. A woman of wisdom, compassion and gentleness. She looked across the land and saw a shadow of a girl among the trees, knowing it was Kenina. She sighed with great labour. "My dear if only you could find a place to show your true self, you wouldn't have a need to hide or to outwit."

Kenina shivered a little from the tree line as autumn was beginning to present itself. She moved slightly further into the forested brush to avoid her mother's eyes. Her plans, she felt were written on her face, so she turned away.

Meanwhile, in the family hut, the brothers began to become aggressive in their terrorising state, mother Lilith backed into the shelter hoping to avoid being another victim of their power. Completely unpredictable and irresponsible, they filled her with dread. A feeling she was almost ashamed by.

Just as mother Lilith was sure she would be tonight's

victim of impugnity, a loud warrior's battle bugle sounded from the East of the city. It was piercingly loud and disturbing. Many people in Emrun began to panic and either run away or fetch any weapon they could. Broomsticks, knives, swords. All three of Kenina's brothers became frantically enraged. Could it be that the city they had just conquered was already attempting to seek revenge? Each brother gathered their swords and spears hastily and rushed away leaving their mother still cowering away, wiping briefly escaped tears with shaking hands. Her quivering made this attempt messy and her hair became stuck to the tears on her hands and face. Knowing not who had come to attack the city, she just awaited fate, enjoying a moment of silence and feigned serenity.

Kenina finally entered the hut, cheery and unbothered. She whistled a simple tune and the breeze was delighted to carry it. Mother Lilith was surprised at her daughter's calmness at first, until she noticed that under her fur coat, was a battle bugle. In anticipation of the callous state of affairs, she had in fact deceived her brothers into thinking that an army was approaching, in order to buy her and her mother a night of peace.

"Kenina it is not good what you have done, but I remain grateful. I do wish that you would marry and leave this city. For our sake." her mother expressed.

"Mother there is no man near here that has a heart of truth. No man is worth the submission of body, when his mind is a dominion of terror." Kenina retorted sternly. Her mother's eyes were fixed to the ground as was her hope. "There is only one thing I know, Kenina. Your protection of the forests, planting trees, raising young animals and repairing homes after fires will always earn you favour with the gods of nature. Perhaps the wilderness will be your greatest protector." Mother Lilith knew of something deeper than Kenina did. Kenina felt somehow that there was no darkness to be found in the wilderness unless she were to carry it in her own heart.

The sun was low in the sky and whispering its' "See you again" to the horizon. Before the two women decided to prepare to sleep, Kenina layed a small amount of meat outside of their hut, knowing that wolves would come to indulge. They never caused her harm, but for as long as she could hear them outside, she knew her brothers were far away. Deceptions and tricks had become her method of survival. Although benign today, there was a capacity to outwit anything. After all, many people speak of the Machiavel who destroys, but they have never understood the Machiavel who has no choice.

"As darkness sweeps across the eyes, the sounds of wolves do arise. The great gods of the forest guarding them all. But if you should cross before their sights, oh daughter of fire you too shall arise - for the gods are in you after all." Mother Lilith sounded the ancient poetry as Kenina passed into slumber. Wondering if she would ever understand.

CHAPTER 2:

Emrun's Embers

The red skies of a peaceful evening became the gargling cries of morning. Kenina was awoken by calamity. Noises from every direction; wailing, screaming and terror. Her hut glowed red and orange and she dragged her slowly waking mother out into the open. Smoke billowed from every direction and her throat became as if hot ash had lined it with the strongest spices. Coughing, her mother pushed her away. "Kenina, this is your brother's doing. I am assured. You must escape to the forest. Hide there and don't come back for a month!" Lilith was almost screaming through her own layered lungs.

"Mother, you must come with me!" Kenina was shaking her head frantically.

"I have three sons missing in the flames, my duty is to salvage what I can and seek their safety. But you must go alone where you will be safe!" Her mother pushing Kenina still, but ever weaker. People of the city were stumbling past in all directions, but Kenina saw only her mother in the slowest of motions.

Kenina held onto her mother and attempted to drag her away but she was unwavering in her pursuits. Eventually she couldn't breathe well enough to stay and she felt close to losing consciousness. In a final decision to respect her mother and attempt to remain alive, she departed, quickly running deep into the nearby forest.
"No city has ever taken revenge like this." A person called but Kenina knew not who it was.

The burning sienna flames followed Kenina into the thickly endowed forest, creeping along with roaring heat and power. But as Kenina ran deeper into the forest she realised that it was in fact raining extraordinarily heavily and she couldn't understand how the flames were still climbing. She was strangely overcome with confusion. So much confusion, that she suddenly stopped to look behind her to gather an understanding of the situation. Only to see the flames disappear into non-existence. Deep in unknown territory, Kenina scanned the depthy woods. An endless expanse of cooling, shaded enchantment. There was an unusual feeling about this rich forest and it was almost as if Kenina could feel the presence of an ancient magic. Unease was presented with standing hairs. There was a gut tightening will to look over her shoulder every few moments. Kenina trembled to wonder what flame had driven her there. An evil spirit perhaps?

There was a silent calm across this densely entwined forest, but Kenina was weeping bitterly in the strange environment. She crouched down and prayed to whoever was prepared to listen to her plea. Feeling that if she could beg someone in the skies above, they might have an emotion of pity for her nerve shattering predicament of being completely alone and lost. Upon closing the prayer, a small shadowy movement was impossible to ignore. It appeared to have a set of antlers so it seemed reasonable to suggest that there were deer nearby. Shrugging away the shivers about the strange shadow, she began building a shelter of thin twigs and malleable materials found in the woody detritus. Strangely despite the rain, the fire she lit in front of her shelter radiated a great warmth and was not in any state to die overnight. Indeed after all that running and weeping, Kenina was not only lost in this haunting tree filled expanse without a soul she knew of, she was also now soon to lose the sun's friendship until tomorrow. Kenina laid the knives she carried in her fur coat inside one end of her shelter, pulled the coat over her face and began to attempt to find the solace to sleep. After all, darkness would stay for a long while, just as all Autumn nights do.

As the evening continued to draw in and Kenina was almost sleeping, she heard men's voices and immediately lifted her head. They were looking for her, the sister of the devil brothers. They were intent on capturing her. In a state of adrenaline forced survival she clambered nearby, high into a densely vegetated tree. An evergreen.

As the strange warrior men passed beneath her, she noted the names the men were calling each other.

As they split up in search of her, one of the men passed beneath her once more, but this time, alone.

"Are you Arthur?" Kenina called out in a deep, conniving voice.

"Yes, but who is speaking to me? Where are you, disembodied voice?" The man responded feeling thrown.

"There is a man in this forest who goes by the name of 'Arran'. He has vowed to catch you and kill you while you hunt a girl who never existed. Think, have you ever seen a sister of Dub, Dother and Dain?" Kenina pushed her voice even lower, so that it sounded quite sinister.

"How can I believe you strange voice?" The man began to quiver.

"Such things I cannot force. But I wish that you will be wary of he who calls you a friend. For it is not wise to fall to an enemy posing as a comrade." Kenina continued to instil fear in his heart.

In a fit of nervousness, the warrior walked towards the edge of the forest almost out of Kenina's sight just as his companion spotted her in the trees. With chaotic haste he ran towards the other warrior to tell him that he had found her. But distrust had overcome his comrade, due to the twisted words of Kenina. As Arran ran towards Arthur, Arthur lifted his sword to him fiercely and in uncoordinated reaction, the two men landed on one another's swords.

Not wanting to fall foul to the other and step away. The men were brutes, but not much in the way of intelligence. Kenina felt unwell seeing the fatal moment unfold, but sighed with the relief that it was finally safe to return to her shelter. A thought kept playing with her as she slid out of the tree and returned to the shelter. Is this how life would now be? Deceiving and tricking her way into her next breath?

Stars glittered as if to be a frosting, framing the solid flames of Kenina's fire pit. The shelter was warm and quite comfortable considering the hardened ground beneath. Great sadness shrouded the daughter of fire while the rest of the wood rested peacefully. It was disarming to finally feel a second of peace and safety. Grief began to express how heavily it sat in her stomach. For a second it was numbing and empty. But the moon rose high and so came the darker fears to put grief back in the shadows below. A shadow blocked dearest moon's dances for just a moment. Is it possible for a shadow to have a ferocious shape? Kenina grasped her dagger and quickly set her eyes upon the perpetrator outside her shelter. A massive, matted, black wolf with fire for eyes turned to look at her. He growled, snarled and was successfully intimidating. He then began continuing his journey. Kenina knew at once that it was the Shuck of the dead. A lone HellHound who her mother had warned, haunted these forests. Frozen in fear, she felt intensely vulnerable to its ferocity and very exposed with no doors to close.

"He won't touch you. This is simply my warning to you. Never return in pursuit of your mother". A voice sounded from the darkness behind Kenina. "Who are you? Evil spirit leave my home! I have never invited the likes of you and your Ratten Hell-Hounds". She shouted in a vain attempt to intimidate.

As she said this, her fire turned to cold burnt wood.

The cold began to creep into bones and lungs and Kenina huddled into her fur coat to weather the night. She kept her eyes closed even for the moments she awoke in fear, with an anxious determination not to set eyes on anything even more sinister.

CHAPTER 3:

Unwelcoming Voices

Try as she did to relight it, this little pit fire remained stone cold. The rains had fully subsided so it was a mystery as to why it remained so impossible. A breeze howled slightly as Kenina sat in the leaf litter and she shuddered to remember the howls of Shuck the night before. At this point there was no motivation to light a fire anymore. With a deep unease and numb fingers it seemed unattainable. The stillness of her surrender to the situation allowed the memories of her mother in the city flames to return. Kicking her legs slightly as she imagined simply overpowering her mother and dragging her to assured security. Returning to reality became chilling and empty. Her gaze returned to the mysterious pit fire.

"Perhaps the fire in your heart and name will do it". A shadow began to chuckle wryly. "You grossly underestimate your destiny, yet look at yourself, you grossly overestimate your troubles". The shadow did not reveal himself.

"Beast of darkness, you are not welcome. I intend to light this fire for my sanity and you speak to destroy it. My screams are of virtuous anger, not once in fear of the likes of you". Kenina feigned courage to disarm the brazen voice.

"But I've seen what you do here. You trick the men who come to find you. Even to the point of fatality. You take daggers to lone wolves. What makes you think I can leave you unwatched? Does this place belong to you, oh swine of fire?" The shadow began his taunt and his voice became clear. It was a deep voice that brought even savages to listen.

"I can't freeze here," Kenina whispered almost inaudibly. Trying to ignore the shadow play.

"For a soul who is at peace with taking life away, why does she seek to be given it? There are corpsed soldiers at the base of this woods and I hear you set them upon themselves. Oh swine divine, what is your motive?" Although the voice said terrible things, he almost seemed bright and excited.

"Who told you I did that? Where are you, vulgar creature? A coward to conceal himself." Kenina began to drop her cover of courage and swept her eyes across the wooded brushland.

"Your confirmation was my only requirement. Girl of ice, survive the morrow."

Leaves crackled as the shadow disappeared into the brush. Once again, antlers were visible shrouded in fog.

In an attempt to shorten the days' experience, sleeping through the day and also the night was Kenina's only hope. Memories appearing and disappearing as frightening images, both real and imagined danced inside her eyes. It occurred to her that what she imagined was always far worse than the memories. But somehow she felt great comfort in hope that it would prepare her for anything that might go horribly wrong. After all, fear of the horribly wrong had become her closest friend while pining for home.

By the next day, hunger reared and calamitously groaned from her stomach. Kenina couldn't remember when she last satisfied the waning cries of this new acquaintance. An unnerving weakness comes from this kind of deficit of carbohydrates. Tremoring and slightly faint, Kenina knew that her time to remain clear of mind was thinly stripped. Moments like this, magnify the ultimate fear of lone survival. A fear only known to those who have no clear path of escape. No clear route to safety.

Traipsing along a scarcely beaten path, Kenina was shocked to find a pile of headless deer. There must have been more than twenty laying in front of her. In haste she began tearing pieces and gorging on the beautiful meats. Attempting to scoff as much as possible before the owner of the meats might come, Kenina did not hear an approaching figure as she feasted noisily.

"Where is that swine of fire? Stealing meat from the dead and stealing meals from the hungry?" The figure angrily bellowed.

"Reveal yourself! You beast of my insanity. Each time you speak, a piece of my serenity sublimates!"

Kenina threw a leg of meat behind her, hoping to hit the figure. Hunger had presented a defensive anger.

"Oh swine, tread wisely. It angers me to think that you can't respect me." The voice became gentle but cunning.

"Why do you hound me?" She pleaded.

She suddenly felt the warming breath of the shadow against her left ear. "Everyone needs to be satisfied, Little Fire. But sometimes swine take our banquets." The voice began gentle and became more ominous.

She swung around only to see nothing. With impeccable haste, Kenina began to try to outrun the voice. She heard him as she ran, jesting " What will it take for you to come to me, oh trickster I don't like a swine who acts as if I have competition. I can take the souls of thirty deer and yet this human runs as if she isn't going to have to face me. It is my mercy that…". He was interrupted.

"Your mercy is a façade and so are your threats. Get behind me, beast!" As Kenina retorted, the footsteps stopped.

"That statement you'll regret when I come to find you again. Look out for me." The voice chuckled and became quiet.

Thankfully, Kenina had arrived at her shelter… but she knew not how she got there.

CHAPTER 4:

Spitting Images

Nightfall came with an uneasy dryness and the wind was bitter. In the shelter, Kenina pulled her fur coat over her head for fear of ill health in the chilling air. It was almost unusually cold for autumn. Kenina began to imagine what her scene of peace could be. Someone warm to share the space with her. Maybe a person or a little animal. Loneliness surely was the maker of desperation. She wondered what it might feel like to have a man who was kind to the soul and thawing to the touch. But it felt worrisome to consider this, for Kenina knew the capacity of her brothers to bring harm. Perhaps a man would be the same. It seemed best to assume that she would have to fight life alone, but an imaginary gentleman danced in her mind and lulled her to a happy sleep. Meanwhile her whole body shivered.

Many hours later, upon seeing the sun raise its steady head, Kenina slowly felt her body return to warmth and movement. She bashed her feet on hard ground to bring feeling back to them. At the edge of a blackberry bush, a robin began singing a tune Kenina recognised well. The dawn chorus was beginning its hearty blessing to all the gods of Alba, but this robin seemed separate and focussed on Kenina. She whistled back to him and he stayed with her for the duration of her gathering. He continued to serenade sweetly upon her shoulder and made her laugh with his comical character. "A rather typical bird of his kind but with a spirit far bigger than him!" Kenina thought to herself.

"Thank you, oh woods for finally sending good spirits." Kenina tipped her head to the sky, breathed in deeply and extended her gratitude. It seemed finally as if the darkness of the woods had lifted and Kenina wondered if this meant that her city was healing. "Yes, indeed I shall return to Emrun soon" she announced. But soon as the afternoon sank into even the shadowed brush, Kenina noticed the whimpering of a pup only perhaps a month old. He limped along the path behind her. A solemn spirit of weakness. He struggled to lift his head or respond to Kenina's approach. She moved slowly and with gentleness, making only soft sounds to reassure him.

"My god, when an animal appears, it is never alone." Kenina expressed. Without a thought for her berries, Kenina lifted the golden brown pup and wrapped him securely against her chest, covering him with her fur coat. The pup nestled and whimpered. Kenina whispered into his ear, "I promise you pup, whatever you need, I will do for you. Even if it be difficult." She kissed his tiny head with a love that only mothers offer. Instincts of a maternal nature are strong for some. The ability to sacrifice almost anything for a small, struggling soul one has only just met. Turning word into action, Kenina placed him down in her shelter and went about finding him something to eat. As she exited the shelter, she noticed her fire pit was glowing powerfully, which was an unexpected warming of the soul.

Kenina was walking for only a short time before another large pile of deer became visible. It was quite shocking to see a pile like this once again, but without a thought for concern, Kenina knelt down and hastily cut a leg free for her pup and then immediately began running to avoid the owner of the meats. By the time she could see the shelter, her running had slowed to a walk as the woods seemed very quiet. In fact the forest in general felt firmly steeped in a new reality. Excited to present her pup with the meat, Kenina swung into her shelter blindly, only to crash into an extremely tall man standing in front of the shelter. His boots were of thick leather, a brown fur cape covered him from head to toe. Upon crashing into him, there was a clanging sound of a sword under his coat. As Kenina gazed up at his face, she showed a flicker of anxiousness, for his face was stern and unwavering. Not to mention unwelcoming. He wore a helmet of stag antlers that stretched even higher as if to command the sky. She noticed he was not so muscular he could not run fast, but he was the sort of tall, broad man that could easily be a hunter or warrior. Athletic but terrifying. The meat Kenina was holding dropped onto the leafy detritus.

"Where is…the… th.. th" Kenina stammered.

"You couldn't help your sorry soul, stealing from the strong to feed that which will die inevitably and now a little slower." The man spoke slowly emphasising the dark patterns of his speech. His eyes were playing a game for which Kenina did not know the rules. He then stepped slowly towards her with a look of domination. Towering over her, most frighteningly. Kenina took a breath and stood firm in a wave of indignance. He smiled a little. "Is this your big moment? To feel the sweet pleasure of being powerful - Giving and taking where you please? Can a human ever depart from such clichéd obsessions?" His words brought tremor to the floor and taunted the air around Kenina. She raised her head with what thinly veiled confidence she had left and tried to think of her pup.

"I don't care about you, where is the pup…?" She was interrupted sharply.

"As much as your goodness is a façade little swine, so is my illusion." The man was undeterred but suddenly he turned and disappeared into the brush with strong haste and Kenina's fire pit froze over with one swing of his cape. A shudder came to her body as the flash of a silver sword showed briefly from under his cape. There was no pup in the shelter and no robin in the bushes. The voice of the man sounded again, rumbling from a distance.

"What would it take to convince you? To show your dark fire to me, oh swine?" He taunted from a distance. "I know who you are." He added menacingly.
"You can't trap me beast, you might prefer deer." She retorted in fearful frustration.
"If to trap you is to remove your mask, then I think you should attempt your fruitless escape Little Fire." He laughed and laughed. But as time went on, the cold set again into Kenina's bones and tears of loneliness became the only replacement for the hollow glares of emptiness that frequented her sorry heart. The man had completely disappeared and Kenina swore to herself that she would hold firm against the evils of the forest.

Even though this time she had her strategy for weathering the cold, Kenina wept at the thought of having to survive on the brink like this. Remembering her mother's embraces and warm winter soups made it even more heart wrenching. Sometimes she still wondered if she could have done more to keep her dear mother safe but rested in the fact that she could return in less than a month. Kenina had been counting the days by drawing lines into the soil by her shelter but dust had been blown over it and she began to carefully assess the moon each night. There was joy in her heart each time the moon got larger, just awaiting another full moon to give her the allowance to return home.

During the night Kenina prayed often to whoever would listen. Sounds could be heard all around her shelter with every prayer and some came across more sinister than others. Kenina began to change her mind about waiting for a month, for the forest didn't seem like it could protect her in the way mother Lilith had suggested. Perhaps it would be worth trying to find her mother tomorrow. The treacherous journey would have to begin early.

CHAPTER 5:

The Dusky and Dangerous

The Spirit of Fire rose within Kenina at the exact moment that dawn flashed its first oranges and reds, matching the fire pit and contrasting the deep grey that Kenina saw. Her plans to seek out mother Lilith could not come to pass. Such a sudden realisation and a worrying one. Kenina knew this as soon as there were birds singing in the distance to serenade a sunrise she could not see. A dense fog had covered every breath of the woods, leaving Kenina feeling totally lost. She had a strong desire to find any vague constitution of a breakfast nonetheless. Her stomach made noises that she wished it wouldn't, in case something evil had heard her awakening.

To quieten the gut, Kenina began crawling along the forest floor, feeling around for orientation was the only option. Despite her industrious approach, Kenina still found herself hopelessly lost. As soon as a tree root could be felt at her fingertips, Kenina climbed up into the tree to await better visibility conditions. She couldn't see how high she had climbed but considered herself elevated sufficiently to feel slightly safe. Again, she sent prayers to whoever would listen. She wished and begged for protection from the evil and cold. As this prayer ended on the breeze, a pack of vicious wolves surrounded Kenina beneath the tree. Hardly visible, they jumped in and out of visibility. Their barks and snarling marked their presence with definition. Kenina responded in a clear attempt to present her will to survive. She swung at them with her dagger from her high point, yet they remained unfettered and they barked, jumped and snapped with a focussed malevolence. Just as one wolf came within biting distance, Kenina tipped backwards on her branch and was close to losing her balanced disposition entirely. She yelped and pulled herself upright, almost overcompensating. But as this happened, in one single moment, every wolf suddenly whimpered pitifully and escaped into the distance and thick mists. Kenina's heart felt as if it had given up on a rhythm, for she could feel that there was now something stronger than wolves in her midst.

"I'll give you what you wish for, Swine, but you are obligated to keep those promises you throw like dust." a voice sounded that Kenina now recognised.
"I wish for nothing from you! I wish only for you to be gone. I have made no such promises to evils such as you!" Kenina shouted so forcefully that her plaintive spirit caused her voice to break a little.
"Silence!" His bellow almost caused her to jump

from the tree. Discreetly, she clung tighter to the branch to weather another possible fright. The man Kenina now feared most in this forest, marched to the bottom of the lonely branch and he lifted his weighty sword as if it were as light as an oak leaf and pointed it at Kenina with total unmovable steadiness. Kenina was visibly trembling and her eyes were fixed to the spectacle. Unable to avert her gaze. "Every liar in your kin has been destroyed at the hands of hell. Tell me you want their fate. Tell me you are ready to be the fifth. Tell me you don't think I decided it!" The man bellowed each word with frightening definition and his eyes were direct. Unblinking. His Stag antler helmet reached almost to Kenina's quivering toes. Two warrior guards stood between Kenina in the tree and the route to her shelter. They became slowly more visible as time developed. Standing perfectly still with great spears in their right hands, the guards were still not as tall as the sword brandishing brute beneath her.

"Promises like dust? Who have I promised? There is no one else here in this void of trees" Kenina pleaded sorrowfully, feeling completely trapped.
The man smiled, "do you not remember? Or did my whimper disarm you?"
Kenina's mind flashed immediately to the moment that she held a pup in her arms the day before. Thinking of how she had promised to do anything for him and had held him close. A shiver came from the depths.

"No! No! No, that is not viable! You deceived my heart. I thought you were a mere pup in harm's path. You can't enforce this, you beast! I'll say it again, you are a beast! I refuse to be afraid of your evils!" Kenina became hysterical to see his sword still aimed at her despite the words she threw at the air.

"Who ordained you to decide? If deceit causes the thief's heart pain, wait for it to be ripped out!" The man's billowing response was not only shocking but dark in nature and dark in tone.

"You are a monstrous spirit filled with cunning callousness." Kenina sobbed, throwing away the façade of confidence which had betrayed her.

"I sense that at last your judgement is aligning with truth. Don't you think?" The man replied in a quieter tone and lowered his sword. He swung into his turn and began to disappear into the brush. "Wait here swine." Came his final words.

Knowing that tricks would be the solution to unmatched force, Kenina waited until he was completely out of sight, watching the stag antlers fetter into fog. Wasting no time and following the patterns of adrenaline, Kenina let her fiery red hair down and thankfully it still sat beautifully. She then straightened her dress a little with the palm of her hand and slid out of the tree. Continuing to straighten her dress and twist her hair as she approached the two guards. Her only option would be to charm the warrior guards in hope that they were not the brightest of men. This was not something she lacked experience in. Gliding confidently but quickly as she approached, then as her charms took over, moving slowly and daintily. Kenina began the attempt. "You on the left, what is your name?" Kenina spoke very softly to the guard but there was no answer, not even a little flash of eye contact. She very gently pulled on the warrior's sleeve. "Can my interest in you bargain me out of here? Tell me warrior, what are your desires? I promise to fulfil them." The warrior surprisingly began to speak, "My name is Cernunnos." He said as Kenina began to smile at him.

Kenina recognised the name 'Cernunnos' from her mother's stories.

"Cernnunos! You are named after the god of Alba, my mother told me once. He has great stags antlers! Pray tell, what are your desires god of…"

She realised what had happened but it was too late. The warrior shapeshifted into the man who had just left. Kenina knew the man had to be Cernnunos of Alba. A god of enormous capability, but his sinister nature left her terrified. His size was indeed enormous and she now felt her blood of fire, run like ice. How could a god be so terrible? She could feel herself breathing heavily in panic, then began to feel strangely dizzy and begged her body to stay in the present moment for fear she would never have the privilege of waking up. Only feet from him, no longer in her high point, he seemed even larger than last time.

"So many promises, so many bargains." He began to slip his words into the breeze and stepped forward to meet Kenina's gaze. "Too little sincerity, too little respect." He stared down at Kenina as if to have won a deadly game. One she still did not know the rules for. Meanwhile her tremors continued, for Kenina was certain this was her last day to live. This god had a deep set malevolence. The hunger she felt and her fast, panicked breathing caused her to crouch down all of a sudden. Cernunnos kept her gaze and knelt in front of her, with his arm resting on his one upright knee as she dropped. His eyes did not waiver from her and could pierce souls. Kenina tried to look down to avoid his domineering gaze. But once her knees hit the floor, he smiled into her eyes with a hint of enjoyment and she met his gaze without thinking. Feeling that air wouldn't fill her lungs for the moment of terrifying silence he held before her, Cernunnos finally spoke after Kenina gasped.

"This was my desire." Came his words. Still grinning at her. Kenina flung her head up at him, shocked at the god as he stood up slowly. She felt strange. He looked down on her and his stag horn helmet appeared to stretch up to the heavens.

"Take care in the fog next time." He jested before turning and walking away with a certain assertive Marcato, his shoulders swaying slightly with his gait. His head up, surveying the woods. The other warrior fell to dust as if it never really existed. Kenina returned to the shelter. Berries kept the pain away.

CHAPTER 6:

Spirits of War

In the slightly warmer night breezes of that evening, Kenina felt a rush of energy and couldn't submit to slumber. Clarity of mind came strongly and without wondering why, Kenina went in search of her city. Rose hues coloured her memories of Emrun. The dances and smiles. Laughter and embraces. Warm summers and delights. Through the undulating paths she almost skipped. The trips of tree roots in the dark, tried desperately to bring her to Earth. There wasn't a question for where this energy came from, there was no substantial meal before her and no sleep enjoyed. Kenina finally came to the base of the forest where in the distance she could see her beloved city. Out of breath, an ache of the mind was pushed aside by her desire to find her family. There was an unbroken silence above the city. Other than fallen huts and burnt grasses, she could not see any further in the dead of night. Anguish reared as Kenina cried out.

"Was this the view you knew would corrupt my soul mother?" She was desperately catching breaths in between each cry. "This is what you have left behind? When the month is over what do I have to return to? WHAT DO I HAVE LEFT?" Her pleading became defeated. "I could even miss my brothers in the midst of insanity and the ancient cries of laughter in the morning. But could you not have gone with me? Could you not have stayed with me?" The last cries, superfluous.

A man stepped onto 'High Point' and appeared to Kenina from the rubble.
"Kenina? Do I heed an apparition?" He jovially called out as he sat down on an old boulder. Kenina scrambled up to High Point, a slight hill in front of Emrun.
"Kallan! You're alive! Where are my mother and my brothers? Please help me to find them." Kenina was naturally bursting with questions.
"Even Your Brothers of turmoil you miss. Villains of the innocent. You seem certain that you wish to find them as well, is that true?" Kallan seemed a little surprised and cautious.

"Kallan, you have fought many a battle by their side." Kenina felt surprised that he did not see them as she thought he did.
"Some of us have no choice but to master the acceptance of those more powerful." Kallan looked down as he spoke. Make no mistake, Kallan was tall and the broadest of men. A red beard and a bald head. The warrior's helmets tended to pull the hair. His heart was also broad and open. Kenina had often

taken refuge in his words and wisdom. But there was defeat in the eyes of the good.

"But you see, in the forest I have learned many lessons. It seems there are greater problems than the chaos of a family. I feel a hole as if they are gone entirely. What else can I do other than find them? I have reason to believe that survival depends on them. Let us go Kallan, you have always been good to me. Please be at my side once more to seek them out." Kenina had so much to say, but even more that she wished to achieve in that single night.

"Dearest Kenina, I cannot help you. In the depth of my soul it pains me that I cannot. I waited here for you, but merely to wane a goodbye on the breeze. You should stay in the forest much longer. The danger here is great, both from vengeful warriors and the underworld. After some are gone, we feel their departure and miss them. This does not mean that they were fulfilling or pleasant in the flesh, others are to be kept dear Young Fire... and remembered wholeheartedly." His eyes were filled with pain and sorrow as he met her breaking eyes.

"No! No, I cannot go into the forest! I am not safe Kallan, please you must change this, why don't you stand up with me. Why can't I pull you up?" Kenina suddenly felt something was deeply wrong.

"Dearest Kenina, I cannot". Kallan held his hands out to her as he faded into the mist and breeze.

This desolate place from the high point, felt suddenly much colder without Kallans' presence.

Kenina screamed bitterly. Begging him to return. In hopeless fury, she kicked rocks and threw stones at the fallen huts on high point. She stayed there all night, eyes red as embers, eventually resting her head on the stone Kallan had appeared to be sat on. There, she slowly fell into a deep sleep out of collapsed exhaustion.

As Kenina was uncomfortably awoken by the sun's return, her eyes adjusted to the light and it revealed the true desolation before her. Not a piece of the city was standing. In the far distance war cries came from the West and grew ever louder. Gathering the strength to stand, Kenina began running back to the forest. Although some spears came close to where she was, it seemed certain that the warriors had not seen her. Even so Kenina kept up her quickened pace all the way back to her shelter. It was an enormous effort of distance and endurance. She placed her hands on her knees to stabilise her inhalations upon arrival. For once, glad to be back. But upon clearer inspection, Kenina noticed slashes through her shelter and her fire pit was trampled cold. Her small piece of safety had somehow been uprooted.

The hairs on her body stood akin to deer before torches as she sensed a mighty presence.

CHAPTER 7:

Ace of Tricks

As the sun was weakening and dozing, Kenina settled her anxieties in pursuit of sanity, to begin repairing her shelter. The mighty presence that she felt wasn't appearing, so instead Kenina assumed it was simply her fears incarnate. Carefully winding new twigs through its structure, she began rebuilding her safety.

But as soon as peace entered, so did a familiar voice. "It's no use. The night will draw in. You will freeze." He spoke without a care. Kenina dropped her head down and heavily exhaled, realising who it was.

"How can a god like you be so..." Kenina paused. She was afraid of his response.

"So... Clever? Incorrigible?" He laughed.

"Insatiably sadist." Came her answer. Cernunnos pulled his chin down and inhaled sharply almost to jest at her attempt to upset him. He stepped towards Kenina, with a stare that hawks were dethroned by.

"Oh now, don't play your façades of courage." He breathily taunted. "We both know who you are." There was an eery pause as Cernunnos turned his smile to steel. Kenina stood up with a jump.

"No! Stop with your torment! Do you not see how I am living? Haven't you done enough?" She gestured towards the damaged shelter. Cernunnos audibly exhaled in the form of a voiceless chuckle. He then stepped beside her as she once again crouched before the shelter, almost to avoid confronting him.

"You assume I destroyed this shelter of yours? What callous distrust." He slightly softened his voice.

"Leave me alone to fall apart, to perish even." She retorted. "Why don't you aim your sword. I'll jump in front of it!" She continued. "Shred my heart into fine pieces, that I might never bear the curse of feeling! You threaten to remove my life and it is now all too tempting upon the wake of unhealing burns within my soul." Kenina practically snarled as she glared into the eyes she'd once been terrified of. A small twig was all she had to throw in his direction, hoping to rile him.

A moment passed untouched by words, before a sigh came from Cernunnos as he crouched beside her. She threaded twigs, not hiding her tears or her shaking hands, but also stonewalling his friendlier presence. He then looked upon her more compassionately than before.

"You returned to your home didn't you?" He asked with a surprising softness. It began to give Kenina's heart a hope of warmth.

Tears proceeded to overflow in the masses. The sounds of a sobber came uncontrollably from

Kenina's lungs. She didn't want him to see her so unavoidably vulnerable, but somehow the tears flowed in spite. Perhaps because she no longer had a motive to spare herself. After all, what was there to spare?

"My warnings mean nothing to your mind, but perhaps I can offer you a moment of mercy." Cernunnos muttered in her ear. She looked at him a little confused and put her hand to her ear where she had felt strange having his voice so close. She then noticed his eyes had both Hazel and green colours running through them. His eyebrows confidently framed his eyes and his facial structure was well defined. Not to mention that his expression had softened. He was not at all unkempt as Kenina somehow had thought.

"So?" He tilted his head. Upon being plunged back to reality, Kenina darted her eyes away from his and then felt the weakness of her ordeal again. She whimpered,

"They're all gone. Every one of them. I have nothing to return to. Nothing but apparitions of false hope, and identity." All of her words kept coming forward and she hadn't the heart to conceal them. Cernunnos' shoulders were broad and aimed towards her, almost as if to shield her.

"You want to feel safe. To know peace." He gently replied, encouraging her openness.

"I want everything back that I once despised." Kenina wept and continued to open up partly due to his warm disposition but also because of her dire wish to tell someone, hoping that in her desperation these words would be safe. Was it really so that his coat and smell somehow felt like a home.

"Stay close to me little fire, you are freezing." Cernunnos radiated heat and the frosted cold air began to relax around Kenina. His concern gave her the comfort to realise her own deficits. Her tummy rumbled first.

"If you do, will you share with me something to eat? I am afraid of starving." Kenina begged, but as she spoke, his eyes narrowed slightly with caution.

"It seems you will happily take comfort in a god you hardly know. But I am not a slave to your charm. Resting all your trust on me." His reply caused Kenina to look back at him with further confusion.

"Sharing is a deception of the human condition that I am not subject to. To convince someone who has enough, to half his requirements as if it will make another person any better off. Do not sport your manipulations before me. Do not bray pitifully to the gods who know better than to share upon request."

He stood up, the frosted air turned back to ice and all sense of care had sublimated. He was not finished.

"We would never be unburdened of the responsibility to keep supplying those who refuse to gather their own needs and if we ever desisted after once starting, the shortfall would be on our sorry heads according to the brazen souls we rule. Am I not owed that which you have already stolen?" Kenina recoiled as Cernunnos raised his voice and towered once more above her..

"I wanted you to leave and you should heed my plea." Kenina blasted her whimpering voice, losing all will to argue further.

"My warmth to thaw you is not yours to take in a blinding whim, it is mine simply to offer." Cernnunos rebounded, before swiping his cape around in one smooth movement as he turned to leave, lighting the fire pit as he did, but leaving Kenina completely alone and unprotected once again.

Even though the night flew in colder than ever, Kenina was grateful for the roaring flames of her fire pit. She felt an unease about the day's events and the seemingly unrelenting tricks of that godly beast. The few seconds of feigned safety were impossible to fight against and even more painful to have pulled apart by him. She had somehow become an instrument of sadism to this beast. But she couldn't understand how he knew her. Nor why he softened for a moment. Nor why he was so distrusting of a lost girl, barely surviving in a forest. Despite this mystery, the desolation of Kenina's city now remained a penetrating memory of images and thoughts. What could have become of her mother and brothers? The only soul who could answer her questions was the spirit that she trusted the least to give her honesty and the one who seemed to take pleasure in her misfortunes like no other. A soul that might retaliate if he caught her looking for him. A soul that was likely counting her days of life on one hand.

CHAPTER 8:

The Beast and the Fire

The sun's reappearance lit up Kenina's hair like a blaze of heat personified. A reflection of heart and courage. Kenina knew what she had to do and set her face like the hardest flint, to seek out the beastly god of Alba. Not knowing exactly how to go about this, Kenina asserted to herself that this search would somehow be fruitful. As she started wrestling through brush in the direction he'd left, Kenina's mind began processing him. His words over the past days had been very direct with regard to her and even her brothers. There was a definitive knowledge of their evil. His knowledge of her was also startling, for she was not infamous like her brothers. His answers would be Kenina's last hope to understand the relentless position she was faced with.

"Cernunnos? Reveal yourself." Kenina spoke aloud with a tone of awkwardness. "Where can I find you? Do not hide yourself from me. I intend to seek you out regardless of your concealment." Her confidence grew a little. To progress further into the forest she went about scaling the crag of a cliff and promising not to look down until she reached the top despite a number of slips and scrapes. Upon reaching the cliff edge and pulling herself over it, Kenina called out, "God of Alba, where are you?" But, now looking down the cliff she had just scaled, realisation struck hard. "Oh this is terrible, how will I get back down?" Her mouth agape. The cliff was not only much higher than she thought, but much steeper. The downward route would be practically impossible. On top of this, she noticed the god's fur coat laying at the bottom of this crag. With a sudden spike of anxiety, Kenina took three backward steps from the cliff edge. It seemed quite suddenly to be a grave decision to seek this spirit out. What was she thinking? Before Kenina had recovered from the regretful panic, a hand came from behind her and covered her mouth. The person held her tightly around the waist and had an almighty strength.

"Who sent you here?" His voice growled. Kenina yelped but didn't speak. He dragged her to a clearing and pushed her away from him. "I said, who sent you here?" He shook his head and moved towards Kenina again with pace. "Don't start your little tricks - you won't survive the consequences oh deviant sister of evils!" Cernunnos' eyes were locked onto Kenina's with an Eagle's concentration. His hand now grasping a concealed sword. Kenina grasped courage from her depths.

"I have come of my own volition." She began. "But not in submission to your intimidations. I want you to state your explicit reasons for your wish to torment me. Tell me what I have done to you. Tell me why my family are seemingly no more and I am spared only for your torturous gain. I am asking for your unabridged directness." Her face felt red from adrenaline and purpose.

"Did no one tell you that I am your god? You, sister of Dub, Dother and Dain. The ones who have brought nothing but terror to Alba. Do you think I will assume there is no malice to a master of deceit like you? Others may not see your actions, but I have seen them all. Do you not wonder who brought your brothers to demise?" Cernunnos' response was direct and devoid of tact.

"Then why have you spared me?" Kenina was still fearful but confused.

"My father, the great god of Alba insisted I spare you unless darkness were to run through your veins. I agreed only because you have no actions to qualify you to succumb to the hell hounds, but your tactical capacities must show their control if you are to enter the heavenly realms." He stepped forward and looked down at Kenina. His helmet of antlers reaching higher.

"You killed my mother." Kenina said and swallowed with difficulty.

"I wasn't sent to deal with her, I was sent merely to destroy the city of your brothers and isolate you from the aftermath." He dismissed her.

"But you hate me." Kenina pressed her face forward towards him with a bitter expression. Before Cernunnos unveiled his battle sword.

"If I see a moment of your brothers in you, I will stop at nothing to ensure that you don't survive to be raised up to the heavenly realm. I don't have the trust my father has in your so-called destiny, I fear my distrust is not misplaced." His sword flashed a little as the sun caught it. Cernunnos crossed it in front of him, pushing it into the soil and leaning on it. Kenina remembered to breathe.

"Why can you not give me a moment of your eternal life to understand me?" Kenina pleaded.

"You have a month don't you? Prove to me that you are worth sparing." He then looked above her into the distance.

"Why should I do that for a sinister spirit like you?" She questioned him testingly with a grizzly expression.

His face dropped to meet her eyes immediately and he reached forward, straightening her coat's collar with his inhumanly strong hands. He pulled her closer and she was up against the sword standing alone in the mud. Kenina felt as if she couldn't breathe. His hands were far too close to her neck for comfort to be possible.

"I'm watching you. Every breath, every deviant moment. I will wait with great patience to see your evil fires raise their heads and when they do, I will not spare you for a moment." He smiled underneath eyes of piercing focus.

"Then I will stay right here with you." Kenina threw her words into his very face.

"What?" He screwed his face just a little.

"It'll make your job far simpler. I will go where you go. I will discover the questions of my family's fate for myself. Yes, I will wait with great patience for you to tell the story." She straightened her stance.

Cernunnos stepped back and swung his hands out.

"Very well Little Fire, if you are so certain of your goodness. But remember that your promises to me are binding in my presence." He was intrigued by the power Kenina had handed him. Kenina responded.

"I never made those promises to y…" She stopped as his eyebrows raised.

"Finish your speech, Swine of Fire. See what will come of your deceptions." Cernunnos pulled his sword out from the earth and set it again under his cloak.

"If I can't pull tricks, neither can you." Kenina bargained sharply. Cernunnos looked down at her with a tilted head and a smile.

"I have not my viability to prove." His words made Kenina clench one of her fists in frustration. He beckoned to her with his hand as he walked backwards, "Come with me, Fire."

The two souls trekked a long distance and there were, of course, more cliffs to scale. Kenina felt as if Cernunnos was deliberately leading her to difficult places because she had no choice but to keep following him in such unknown territory. Rocks began to loosen beneath Kenina and she slipped, cutting her leg. She shouted a wordless expression and Cernunnos reached out, grabbing her arm tightly and pulling her onto the cliff top. Saying nothing, he continued walking and Kenina plaintively limped after him. It was a feat to keep up with his gait. At times he was very far in front of her, but Kenina mustered the capacity to keep following. Eventually, in one painful moment of discomfort, Cernunnos was almost no longer visible and Kenina considered hiding away to avoid the trek. As the thought crossed her mind he turned around to look at her. A knowing smile filled his expression.

"Is the woman of promises reconsidering?" His tilted head made Kenina feel a sense of frustration once again, but she had no choice other than to follow him and was a little nervous of his possible capacity to mind read. Nonetheless, they didn't have far to go before they had reached a prime hunting spot. There were deer from East to West. The pair hid in a camouflage of brushland and Cernunnos fired his arrows into the clearing. With impeccable aim, he slaughtered as many as he wanted.

"Are you really going to eat all of this?" Kenina was stunned.

"Who told you this is all for me?" His eyes did not depart from aiming.

"I thought that you didn't share?" Kenina snickered slightly.

"Hounds don't have the capacity I do." He replied. Kenina thought that this seemed rather benevolent considering his previous words.

He soon released another arrow and turned to Kenina. "That one is for you. In the light of day I can see that your remarks about starvation may have been honest." His voice remained low in tone to avoid revealing his cover.

"Thank you." Kenina whispered as she looked down, wondering if she did in fact look unwell. Cernunnos placed down his bow for a second and softly pushed Kenina's chin up with his index finger. He was very strong but Kenina could only feel a gentleness in this gesture.

"I won't have a weak spirit follow my path." Cernunnos spoke softly. Kenina felt a strange sensation in her stomach and heart. Almost as if a sparrow was fluttering inside her. She knew nothing of a sensation or feeling like this, so assumed it was the strange consequences of hunger.

After hunting, the day became easier. Cernunnos led Kenina to a stream to wash herself and upon finally arriving at his camp, he began to cook meats for them both. He smiled to himself as his curiosity about Kenina grew stronger, wondering how she could be so spirited and courageous but somehow endearing. He breathed in assertion and exhaled caution while he made a mental reconnaissance of his duty to her naïveté.

"I thought there would be other spirits here."

Kenina remarked.

"Not for now. Your city is in peril so we have removed all spirits to the heavenly realm. Only Morrigan remains over the city and I remain here in the forests. But you must not visit Morrigan for she is ordered not to reveal herself to you. She sent you an apparition of your friend to warn you away a few days ago. It is important that you do not return because of the terrible job she must carry out." He explained and Kenina nodded in understanding.

"Where must I sleep, my legs are heavy from our climb." She asked as she sat beside the fire pit.

"Little fire, you can join me in my shelter. In my shelter, battle is impossible. A great magic wards it. You can't play any tricks there. Join me in all this safety." He walked over to it and beckoned her to look at it.

"Oh no I mustn't…" Kenina remembered a lesson from her mother.

"Mustn't…what? I'm listening." He appeared almost to be laughing.

"Already you make me nervous. It's as if you're in my very mind, but I shan't depart from my mother's suggestions and wane for such confusions." Kenina was very assured of her stance.

"What did you say?" He strode over to her, grinning.

"You, you heard me exactly." Kenina stammered as she felt an unease.

"Of course I did. I heard every moment. I want to hear you repeat that for my indulgence. I'm in your very head? What power." He responded as he knelt beside her.

"My words are not yours to take in a blinding whim, they are mine simply to offer." Kenina rebutted.

He drew her chin towards his with his index finger, just as gentle as before. "Yes." He breathed. "Even my clichés." Kenina pulled her chin away and there was no resistance. She looked away at the fire and could feel him gazing upon her for a few moments before retiring to his shelter to sleep. Kenina snuggled into her fur coat by the fire and slept without shelter for the night. She tried to keep her thoughts clean of him and his strange behaviours.

CHAPTER 9:

The Test of Heart

Morning dawned merely as a flash, before Cernunnos began waking Kenina from her slumber. He handed her some meat and berries insisting that she prepare to leave. Kenina was quizzical and dazed.
"We have somewhere important to go today." He told her. In fact, he seemed positive and his demeanour was inviting. Kenina found herself positively intrigued and readied herself to get moving.

As they started their new trek into the woods, his beckoning was almost alluring. This time he did not walk so far in front of Kenina. They engaged in jovial discussions and ate berries together as they walked. He told her stories of his childhood in the heavenly realms, the horses he would ride across glistening meadows. He came across as if his guard had lowered in totality, in between taking her arm and helping her over difficult meshes of brush. Kenina had the chance to smile and even laugh a little at his charismatic descriptions. It was a moment of openness in Kenina's mind. She also noticed that he was not carrying his sword. He saw her notice his swordless belt and steadied his gaze on the path ahead with a look of seriousness for a moment. Kenina began to tell stories of her childhood in the glens, raising small animals and cooking soups with her mother. They had come from very different places but she felt more alive being able to share her precious moments. The brush was steadily thinning and the forest opened out into a vast plateau. Kenina looked amazed but also concerned.

"We're not going to cross the whole plateau are we?" She couldn't imagine it, especially as the other side was not visible. Cernunnos continued walking steadily and did not answer. Kenina followed on, but dragged behind in a wave of distrust. Having hiked for a fair way, the sun was higher and more pervasive by now. A fair way across the plateau, they were past turning back in a few brief steps. As Kenina began to feel her legs getting heavy from yesterday's walking and now today's, a wild beast came charging towards the pair. A grizzly sight of a mighty bear. It had its mouth open and was not prepared to stop for any man or god. Thinking hastily, Cernunnos ran towards it with all his speed and sounded a battle cry to the breeze. Kenina ran behind Cernunnos, trying not to be isolated from him by the bear. But as the bear reached him, Cernunnos' feet slipped in the wet muds beneath and the bear looked to prepare to jump on top of him. Kenina was not far away and without thinking of anything else, she threw herself on top of Cernunnos, holding his head in her hands as she cried out.

"No! You foul bear! Leave him alone!" She continued to wail. "No! Please no!!" Her cries still came. "Please, bear, he's all I have." Eventually, she calmed her terror and became aware of the stillness around her. She was nervous to look down at Cernunnos who was staring up at her smiling. His stare seemed to reach down through her eyes and into the depths of her soul and presence of self.

"Good Girl." He uttered in an alluring tone.

Kenina could not understand the feeling that came upon her as he said this, so she attempted to stand up and look for the bear. Cernunnos held her still against his chest. She continued to crane her neck around. There was nothing anywhere. He chuckled and took her attention. "There is in fact a test you can pass." He remarked. Kenina took a moment to come to the realisation of his illusion.

"Oh god". She whispered.

"Yes?" He answered.

"How could you do this? Let me go." She scolded.

"I am not holding you." He added. Upon the realisation that he had in fact let go of her, Kenina bolted upright in anger.

He slowly came to match her stance.

"Why would you do such a thing? Convincing me that there was a bear after you!" Kenina complained, ready to burst.

"How else can I know, if you would throw someone

before a bear in a final attempt at deception and greed? Come, let us keep walking." He described his twisted test without apology.

Kenina raised her hand with all of her might and slapped his chin as hard as she had the capacity to muster. It felt suddenly to have been a very bad idea once executed. After all, he didn't come across as easily intimidated. Kenina stood tall to maintain what was left of her conviction to lash out. His eyes lowered to look at her with a look of surprise and stifled a smile. This threw Kenina off completely. He was largely unaffected by her attempt and clearly found it a little charming. Kenina knew how to cope with rage before her, but this response was entirely new.

"I suggest you keep your palms to yourself, Little Fire."

He warned her sternly but in a hushed, light tone. His face still not matching his words.

"Or WHAT?" Kenina shouted at him. With no idea what the appropriate response could be.

Cernunnos took her hand and placed it where she had slapped him and met her gaze with sincerity.

"Or you're going to drive me crazy." He muttered. Cernunnos' eyes still looked through Kenina, but there was a different meaning now that she still didn't understand.

"What? You'll hit me too?" Kenina questioned, looking a little plaintive, hoping he wouldn't agree.

"No, something much better." He whispered and breathily chuckled. This statement left Kenina feeling terribly confused and unsure. As he dropped her hand, Kenina found herself disarmed by his softened disposition and remarked in a hushed tone.

"I was trying to teach you a lesson." She looked away as she spoke. He immediately responded.

"Oh darling, teach me again! Perhaps I'll learn the second time!" His voice was now louder and jovial. Kenina turned away from him with her arms firmly folded and headed back to their camp alone.

Upon arriving at the camp, she knew not what to do for nerves. It was strange to be in such close proximity to a god she once feared most. Nonetheless, she was glad to have been bold in his presence whenever possible. It was a case of waiting for his next unsavoury move, or so Kenina wanted to think. Her mind played very different scenes. Before long, leaves crackled behind her seating place at the fire pit. Kenina turned quickly to see that it was simply Cernunnos.

"You have far more to your character than I had known. It's making me curious." He declared.

"How long have you been standing there?" She quizzed.

"Eat something." He softly commanded, pointing to the remaining meats.

"Did you follow me here? I mean, thank you, it's a little worrisome to be alone. Although, I'm not sure if I trust…" Her words were interrupted.

"Kenina, I do not wish to handle your collapse. Eat something." He demanded.

She nodded and began to indulge the deer meats and legumes. After all, she was very hungry, and the food was indeed delicious. As she indulged, Cernunnos kept disappearing out of the corners of Kenina's eyes. He was busy collecting kindling. But Kenina began to feel strange every time he seemed to disappear into thicker areas of brush.

After a while, Kenina's gaze would naturally scan the area in search of him every few seconds and whenever she regained her senses, Kenina would drive her gaze back to the floor. It felt unusual to be focussed on someone else.

"This Little Fire should keep looking down. It is wise, don't you think?" Cernunnos spoke, but Kenina couldn't work out where he was. Before long, a rustle came from the West and Kenina looked up to see nothing. Then a rustle to the East arose and she became tense with apprehension. Where was Cernunnos? Could she handle a lone wolf on her own? Then, a louder rustle ahead of her behind the fire, caused Kenina to stand up quickly, only for Cernunnos to grab her from behind, holding her waist as she almost lost her footing.

"I'm here, I'm always here." He breathed quietly by her ear and Kenina felt it run through her silently. She lost inhibition for a breath and surrendered her weight to his arms, before she gasped, returned to her senses and pushed him away. Glaring with intent to intimidate.

He stepped forward again and jested.

"If you continue to look upon me like this, you'll find yourself thinking of me very differently." These words surprised Kenina, but she noticed that she couldn't avoid his gaze, for her eyes did not respond as she wished. She began to breathe heavily and her legs felt weakened. This must be another consequence of hunger, surely? Cernunnos leant into her, grazed his mouth against her ear and whispered, "mere seductions, the simplest of human manipulations." Then turned his face to meet hers directly, which was a lot closer now as a result. "You didn't think I'd fall, did you?" He muttered adorning that smile. Cernunnos then stood straight again and immediately left her alone, to retire to his shelter. Now that he was gone,
Kenina's legs swiftly buckled and she flopped onto the leafy floor. There was a strong desire to follow him to his shelter, but she did not heed it.

Kenina didn't understand her feelings as she had never been subject to them before, nor had her family ever thought to mention. Her mother never thought that Kenina cared for such things and her brothers only spoke of war. The people of Emrun didn't dare play with a Daughter of Fire, but Kenina knew nothing of this.

Trying to sleep was difficult, Kenina's mind repeated every moment that she and Cernunnos had come into close contact. She couldn't understand why the moment he grabbed her by the fire pit caused her to feel as if all her fears had finally been put to rest and her body had relaxed into his security. A relief to be in his arms had been so overpowering, before she pushed him away. Yet, when he walked away and left her in the night's unfriendly hands, it was as if her heart had been dragged away with him. Kenina considered running away to avoid these emotions that she could not fathom, but decided to remain at the fire pit for a second night. Not knowing where else might be safe.

The night was very cold and the fire grew dim. Kenina shivered and contemplated her mind's wanderings further.
"Why should I want to be close to he who hates me? Why do I think of him like this? Why, it must be the cold. It couldn't be anything else. Yes, the cold." She spoke aloud without thinking. Yet the heavy feeling in her heart remained since his departure. Her immaturity shone as a beacon. "Has he taken my heart? Why does it feel pulled? Is this what it feels like to have your heart…" She paused.
"Stolen?" Cernunnos spoke and broke the frosted air.
She turned to him with a look of deep concern.
"I might have it in here perhaps." He lightly chuckled while pointing at his shelter.
"What have you done to me?" Kenina pleaded and ran to him confused, but secretly relieved not to be alone. She narrowed her eyes and starkened her gaze to hide her gladness. Cernunnos sighed over his smile.

"This could be a trick of yours, it could be a distraction." He held a pause. "Or perhaps am I the distraction?" He remained cryptic to Kenina. He also wasn't wearing his helmet of stags horns. Dark brown hair sat on his head well collected.

"I don't understand." Kenina mumbled and stepped backwards.

"Really?" He strode towards her and slid his arm across the small of her back while keeping her gaze with the most caring of faces. "Tell me everything you feel." He drew her in as he spoke. Kenina could only just hear him as her heartbeat thumped.

"I-I-I can't breathe." She stammered.

"I'm listening" he whispered as he pulled her even closer. His eyes were starlit, which made him a glistening guardian that Kenina simply couldn't resist.

"My heart, I can feel it's there." She timidly announced.

"Tell me how it feels." He encouraged her to arouse his desire with a deeper description as his eyes further settled into mildness. Kenina felt her voice dampen and hush to match his.

"It's beating so heavily it's…" She couldn't continue as he pulled his body up against hers.

"Do you wish I'd be even closer?" His whisper was so quiet, but far from weak. Almost as if he was drawing her in with a hypnotic force.

"Yes…Oh no I shouldn't be saying such…"

Cernunnos enveloped his arms around Kenina and kissed her. Although he latched on with great sensual confidence, he steadily muted his pressure to draw her further in. Kenina's body was only standing because of his embrace and she was overtaken by bliss, at least for a second before returning once more to her senses.

"Oh god help me" She pleaded as she pushed him away.
"With what?" He asked.
"No, I meant..." She couldn't form a sentence. Cernunnos clasped the sides of her coat and pulled her back towards him. With seductive draw, he appealed to her.
"Tell me what you want Kenina. What do you desire?" His nose now tracing hers.
"Let me go, I need my sanity." She retorted. He let go without any resistance to prevent her.
"You don't even know what this feeling is, yet you are so quick to demolish it. Is this submission of body so terrible? Is your distrust so great?" He remarked as he could see the oppression with which she caged her mind. Kenina was the one to step forward this time.
"You have never trusted me. I shouldn't need to fall to any force of yours." She challenged his remark.
"Oh but you are wrong. Have you no idea? It has been a delight to see you prove yourself to me." Cernunnos left her with his revelation and left for his shelter once more.

Kenina crouched down into her coat in front of the fire pit and closed her eyes in an attempt to force an immediate sleep. Cernunnos appeared from his shelter for a fleeting moment to starken the warming flames of the fire.

CHAPTER 10:

Deadlock

The next morning the fire burned more strongly than ever before. Yet, the wind had become icy and took Kenina's breath. She made clouds with her exhalations. Even so, birds began to chirp and the world seemed beautiful. The thinnest layer of frozen dew brought out the green in the eyes of every blade of grass. Misty hazes were scented like pine and Kenina felt a great peace. To warm herself, she got up and began collecting berries nearby when she suddenly remembered the happenings of the night before. Flashes of memories that she wasn't awake enough to feel anything for. Yet they appeared in droves. But of course, as Kenina's mind continued to wake up, strong emotions flooded her consciousness. She wondered if it was wise to run away to avoid these feelings, but although she had the capacity, Kenina couldn't bear being away from him. She was split between fear of this god's capacity and being drawn in by the tension that she wished he would keep creating.

The sun was steadily rising, plenty of berries were collected for the day and Kenina went to a nearby stream to bathe herself carefully. She found herself thinking often about how Cernunnos would look at her, hoping somehow to keep his attention - though she knew not how. Each comb of her hair in the cool waters and each swipe of her face almost felt important. Logically, she feared this god and felt that his disposition was unpredictable, but her heart's curiosity was taken by him. Not to mention being consumed by the thoughts of his actions and words. Each instant that he had been close to her, played in her head as if to be a new hobby. Having lost everyone around her made the occasional warmth and closeness of him even more compelling and enthralling. It felt as if practically nothing could harm her while he distantly kept watch.

Kenina put on her garments and walked slowly back to the camp, taking time to pick autumn blooms and feel the icy cobwebs between trees. It was a moment of dear pleasantry and one she knew was cherishable. Her boots held in hand, to feel the world around her most honestly.

Upon arriving at the camp, Kenina called out to Cernunnos.
"Good morning! I've just been to the stream, what a beautiful morning indeed!" There came no answer but she continued, "the day is beautiful for whatever you've planned! But let us not discuss the night

before, it is better that we simply continue without returning to it." She felt comfortable dismissing it in confidence. But soon it was very strange that she received no response. "Did you leave to go somewhere while I washed?" There was simply a silence. She walked to his shelter and considered for a moment. "He could be anywhere, and it seems he does not want me to know." Kenina turned her head to look around, but her eyes fixed back onto his shelter. "He may not have wanted me to know where he is, but I am not ignorant of deduction. By seeing what is missing from his shelter, I shall know if he is hunting or something else. If I see his bow and arrows are gone, it will be clear." She stood proudly and said, 'He has never shown me the shelter before, but only because I declined. Besides, what he does not know will not anger him."

In one movement, Kenina threw open the woven curtain to his shelter and there sitting on the end of his bed, was the occupier of her mind. His face was stern, but also not emotionally transparent. She felt immediately uneasy, knowing that what she had done was secretive. Cernunnos' eyes remained steady and fixed to hers. Kenina wondered if she should apologise for encroaching, but it seemed as if it might be superfluous because he would have heard her words outside the shelter.
"Come here Kenina." Cernunnos beckoned her in a low tone. His hand gesturing the same. Kenina worried for she knew not what he was planning to do.

She contemplated running, but outrunning him was never going to be possible from this distance.

Kenina held her breath and walked slowly to him with her hands clasped together and her head tilted down to avoid this ambiguous gaze of his. This god had a habit of drawing her in, but she was apprehensive of his intentions. Kenina stood no more than a foot from Cernunnos and he beckoned again.
"Come closer, Kenina". He spoke even lower in tone. Kenina gingerly took another step forward and her heart began to beat more strongly. It felt as if she was at his mercy, there was no escaping his retaliation. He quickly pulled her into his lap in one clear movement and Kenina realised just how strong he was whilst in his grasp. He had her almost tilted back, but she couldn't grasp the purchase to sit upright with her legs now draped over his other arm. With a gentle inhalation he spoke, "Tell me Little Fire, why you have come to me?" He gazed more gently. Kenina knew that he had heard her outside the shelter and they both knew what she had done. Still, she felt embarrassed to admit it so close to him. Her face became hot and red. Catching a passing breath she replied. "I- I thought you were away, so I simply came to see if you'd gone hunting." She tried to downplay her strong emotions in his arms. He began to smile and exhale strongly before whispering into her ear, "I believe the correct words are, 'I missed you." He pressed his nose into her cheek and then looked in the direction of the shelter entrance

before continuing, "I have no intention of going anywhere today. We have all the meat and other requirements to last us. But you can stay here with me and hear the birds serenade today's sky." There was an air to his words that captivated Kenina. She nodded gently to agree and nuzzled her face into his clothes, for it somehow made her feel secure for a moment, especially as her nodding felt like admitting to something. Her face naturally hid itself. Cernunnos adjusted his sitting to be more relaxed and angled them both slightly back. Kenina's face timidly moved up to look at him sheepishly. Her eyes catching glimpses of his mouth as she remembered the night before. He could tell, but continued looking into the distance. Then she piped up.
"What did we do? What happened between us?" Cernunnos stifled a chuckle and looked back into her eyes.

"Do you mean when we embraced?" He quizzed.
"No." Kenina replied and tried to sit upright again to no avail "I mean…"
"Tell me what it is you are thinking of." Came his reply.
"We did something and I can't name it." She didn't have the words.
"Are you sure we did something?" His reply came as a surprise.
"Yes! I'm quite sure! You must remember it! You pressed your lips into mine and you held me ever so tightly. There was a moment like that and my

legs lost their power, though I don't know why. Oh you must remember!" Kenina pushed her palm against him and looked wide eyed in seriousness. Cernunnos raised his hand and grazed it against her cheek and then came to an affirming grasp behind her neck, gently extending his fingers to grasp more of her hair with it.

"Do you want me to do it again?" His face was now close to hers. Kenina found her mouth agape and didn't reply. He lowered his eyes to her mouth and drew her face closer.

"Do you want me to do it again?" Cernunnos muttered in a hushed tone. His breathing became stronger and his other hand wrapped gently around her waist, tightening to support her.

"Please," came her breathless reply as Cernunnos began to kiss her softly on her lips, mindful of her fragility and apprehension. He deepened and lengthened his kisses to share his rich emotion for her. As they continued, he began to migrate his kisses to her neck at the speed that matched her increasingly confident breaths and Kenina began to relax into this new found pleasure in the safe space he was carefully generating. But she suddenly gasped for air as Cernunnos began slowly sliding his warming hand along her thigh. He kept her gaze with eyes of love and protection as he continued, pulling her skirt up with it. Then he stopped and looked at her with deepest arousal. "I want you to undress and lay inside of my bed. If you want to know what I can do to fulfil your desires. Let me guide you my fire, and show you what you can feel." He spoke with a seductive, alluring tone.

Kenina questioned him, "what will you do with me there?" She found herself turning her remaining fear into excitation.

"I will relieve the yearnings of every part of you that desires me and I will consummate my guard over you. I will make you forget about every part of this world for a time. Your thoughts will only be of me and my thoughts will only be of you." His words were now clearly enunciated and dripping with allure. The seductive forces of this god were unmatched. His presence was deeply and wonderfully powerful. The emotion and heated sensual air around them drove Kenina's desire deep into her emotional fabric and into her bones. Every part of her body began to feel sensations that she craved to feel more of and she finally nodded to him before undressing herself. All the while huddling tightly into his strong, capable arms. He embraced her as she did, hiding her in his arms covered by his cloak, then stood up and placed her inside his bed, undressing himself with ease before joining her there. Under the bear fur blankets Cernunnos pulled Kenina towards him, kissing her with perfect intensity and then he brought her closer that night than any other could and in a way she had never known.

CHAPTER 11:

The Stoat and the Rabbit

The whole day Kenina remained in Cernunnos' divine embrace and held onto him. The night was the same. She couldn't imagine him leaving her for a second. He seemed to wholly appreciate her delicate and close presence. He could also feel her emotional strength as she clung onto him without a thought for anyone else in the world.

Cernunnos looked at his belle as she rested her eyes and began to consider their actions. As he gently stroked her hair and rolled the fiery strands between his fingers, he realised the seriousness of the crux he now had - an Achilles heel.

The only weakness to his impenetrable strength was sleeping next to him blissfully, embracing his safety. Knowing that he now had a strong desire to protect and to love Kenina, he realised that his guard was down and she was in his heart. The best he could do was hope that she was in fact the beauty he could see and not a wolf in a damsels' dress or at least her skin. It only took a sneeze from her after his bear rug tickled her nose for him to smile and feel nothing but adoration. Kenina awoke soon after, stretched out and smiled up to him. She had never felt so safe. She now saw him differently. As a protector and someone very dear. Someone she could not imagine losing. She had to hope that in reality he too had a heart of goodness and not illusion. Kenina was surprised by the depth of feeling she had and felt hopeful that her young rush of emotions had not been an irresponsible act of haste.

Cernunnos looked into the distance and swallowed markedly. Realising the implications of his actions on the Kingdom of the Heavenly Realms, which could spark tribulations for him and his love in times to come. Something Kenina knew nothing of and something that he should have told her. Something that would reveal everything to her. Something that could prove deadly.

Cernunnos of Alba knew what he would have to do.

Soon as morning broke, Cernunnos finally left the bed and began clothing himself in heavy clothes and armoury. Kenina had not seen him wear these clothes before. She felt a slight recoil seeing the sword he was now cleaning and how it once had been aimed at her in the trees many days ago. He placed his helmet of antlers over his sleek locks of hair and suddenly looked much larger somehow. Kenina plucked up the courage to ask him what he intended on doing. But his facial expressions gave nothing away. She slipped out of the bed to ascertain his thoughts. Cernunnos turned to face her with his hand across the entrance to the shelter. Knowing that this could mean he wished to go alone she questioned him.

"How long will you be gone from me?" Feeling solemn somehow. He did not answer for a while.

"You must not leave this shelter until I return." He commanded with grave seriousness.

"But for how lo…" She was swiftly interrupted.

"I am ordering you to stay here where you cannot be found. Stay here where the Magic will ward you. Where I am going, you must not see." He placed his palm against her chest and leant in. "Do you understand my command?" His tone was pressing and Kenina sighed into a nod in response.

He turned, carrying his weaponry under his long winter coat. Kenina noticed that he was leaving footprints in the frost of morning. She watched him leave and head West from the shelter, following with her eyes the majestic warrior whom she now considered her own. His presence was always addictive and Kenina felt a voiding emptiness upon his departure.

An hour or so passed and Kenina had clothed herself and tied her hair back. The feeling of boredom was pressing and Kenina felt sure that her brains could protect her in the forest, besides who could hurt her, the belle of a god? Curiosity for this man she held so dear overtook her senses. Pulling on her boots, Kenina felt prepared to follow his tracks. He would surely be amazed to see her courage to follow him for any hunt. She was not a woman of idleness. There was a tenacity to the spirit inside her. As she set out, the cold did not affect her and there was an air of confidence flowing stronger through the veins. Morning mists were already lifting to show impeccable views.

"Cernunnos should not be afraid to show me such panoramas of the glens. I know them oh so well." She assured herself, despite noticing that the area his footsteps tracked, were through areas she somehow recognised but couldn't quite understand how. The edge of this valley was hanging atop of a steep cliff. The rocks were unstable and Kenina didn't dare scale down this mighty crag. According to the footsteps which reached up to the edge, she knew that Cernunnos must have clambered down the cliff. Her gaze raised up in an attempt to see him in the distance.

In the meadow far below, there were men at battle. But both sides were in panic, as a tall man who they could not see was slaughtering men seemingly indiscriminately. Swinging his swords in delight. A terrifying slaughterer. The people knew not where he was until they were fatally blown by his weaponry. Yet, Kenina could see him clearly disposing of men as if they were deer carcasses. More men came, more men fell. Kenina squinted to see who the devil was and a lump blocked her throat as the flash of deer antlers stretched above his head. Breathing was impossible, but the amount of blood filling the meadow caused Kenina to fall forward onto the frosted ground below, her hands feeling frozen while holding her up from the sweat soaked grass. Dizziness soon left her behind to make way for a response. Terror filled her trembling body as Kenina considered how he had intimately engaged her and tied her up in the most complex and life altering emotions. He had seen her and felt in her in ways no one else had. She had foolishly fallen into the arms of a great demon and of that she was sure. Kenina knew she must be in danger, having been taken in and influenced by him for his own pleasure games.

"What more will he do to me, when I do not have a piece of armour to my name. Nor any force to secure myself from his merciless violence?" Kenina wailed in anguish.

As she said this, Cernunnos swung around, turning his back to the mess of battle and the screaming, hysterical warriors. His eyes did not dance, but they immediately met her gaze. Surely it was impossible to hear her from such a distance as this. Slow and expressionless, he began walking towards her, keeping his eyes locked onto hers. Two warriors in red belts were spared as a result and dashed to a nearby tree line. Kenina, having been able to see him commit these atrocities felt imminent danger rise within her. Quite sure that he would dispose of her in order to guard his name and position in the Heavenly Realms, Kenina began to run blindly into the forests above. Cernunnos was so far away, that

Kenina believed she had the chance to escape him if she fled immediately. Great terror made her exodus calamitous. She scaled gorges and continued for as far as her legs could muster.

With such sprinting came the inevitable stitches and muscle pains. To regain strength, Kenina rested behind a large boulder. It was taller than her, but she crouched low. At first, the world was blurry and air was difficult to get enough of. Kenina kept her focus on recovery. After a while her breathing became slower and Kenina tilted her head up to the sun, hoping for renewed strength from the heavens. At last, she was almost ready to begin running again when a set of footsteps became audible, cracking leaves and sticks. Kenina held her breath and curled up to remain small.

"Do you think that I do not know your whereabouts? Do you underestimate me so greatly?!" Cernunnos' voice bellowed as if to rattle thunder and was devoid of sweetness. Kenina swiftly engaged an aimless dash into the brush. It took might from the depths of her spirit's reserves. Something within us, drives the body on, when the spirit fears the loss of its home. This time Kenina grew tired much more quickly and she stumbled over a tree root. Each breath became painful and freezing. With forceful determination Kenina continued to scramble, bumping into trees and getting caught up in the twine of bushes. But each time that Kenina stopped briefly to regain composure, the footsteps grew louder. Soon, without sufficient time to recover, her vision became distorted with colours flowing and the forest became a disorientating blur. Doubles of trees and doubles of bracken. As soon as her legs collapsed beneath, Cernunnos was upon her without a second of breathlessness. Standing tall above Kenina, he threw his bloodied swords to the ground beside her and picked her up. She hadn't the energy or capacity to attempt to fight his impeccably strong and stable grasp. She lay limp.

Cernunnos shook his head at her.

"Foolish Fire, do you not know? A stoat does not chase a rabbit at his full potential in case of an unprecedented circumstance. Instead with wisdom, he chases it slowly, bringing the frantic mammal to its knees from exhaustion. Do you not think they learnt it from me?" His words did not elicit a response from Kenina for she could only listen, but not muster the strength to argue.

Over the glens and across the gorges, Cernunnos carried Kenina. The walk would have been insurmountable for almost any man. But the godly figure glided as if to be a buck, jumping from one rock to another.

Cernunnos' shelter was a welcome eventual sight and pulling the curtain back, he replaced Kenina on his bed where she had embraced him so sincerely only hours before. By now it was dark and the winds howled with snow in their voices, making his shelter the only place in the Kingdom that Kenina could survive the cold. She slept completely unaware. Her breathing was quiet and Cernunnos found gladness in her unconscious peace. He sat on a stool beside his bed and began cleaning the weaponry he had carried on his back while carrying Kenina. His mind shot back to the moment she looked upon him beyond the battlefield. It seared his heart a little more each time he remembered it. Cernunnos wondered why Kenina had not stayed home.

As he finished their final polish, Kenina stretched and yawned, pulling the bear fur rug over her face which felt cold as she regained consciousness. As she did this, her senses came forth and informed her of where she was. Her first sight was Cernunnos laying his last sword in the corner of the shelter. His helmet lay next to them and his armour was thawing on the floor as snow melted off of it. Kenina was frozen still, partly due to her terrible muscle pains, but also due to her fear of his next move. Would he torture her? Would he keep her alive a little longer for his pleasure before disposing of her? Kenina had heard the stories of her brother's actions of war and the memory became exasperating and upsetting.

Cernunnos came to stand beside the bed looking down at the broken soul laying motionless with an expression of shivering worry. He smiled at her.
"Talk to me. I have a lot to tell you." His words were positively inviting and disarmed Kenina's immediate terror.
She scowled and retaliated against his charm.

"You are a callous murderer, you awful.. awful…". In fear of his possible deadly intentions, she did not finish her sentence.

"I wipe out men who have nothing but destruction in their hearts Kenina." He shook his head.

"Like my brothers." She quickly interjected.

He looked down and breathed in, crouched down to her level and nodded. "Like your brothers."

"You would have taken me." She continued before Cernunnos rose forcefully to a standing pose, inadvertently presenting his height.

"No!" He bellowed and frowned heavily. "Let me never again hear these words from you!" Cernunnos leant over her. "I cannot find even a strand of their evils within you." His shout rattled bones.

"You terrify me. Do you not understand that evil doesn't destroy evil?" Kenina cried.

"A little darkness is required to destroy deep darkness. Did no one tell you?" Cernunnos could not maintain his loud voice at the sight of her sorrow.

"Light defeats darkness." She retorted as he moved to the other side of the bed. Once atop the bed, he placed his hands either side of Kenina's shoulders, coming face to face with her. This caused him to notice the slashes across her body from lone thorns that had grappled with her during her panicked flailings in the brush. It hurt him terribly to see his love in this state, wishing she had heeded his warnings. He addressed her response.

"You say light defeats darkness? Then tell me, will the stars light your path home? No, they are far too dim in all of their glory to battle even the thinnest of clouds. Yet the sun who you think is most glorious, heeds your worship while it burns your very head and skin."

Somehow his twisted responses made sense, but what she had seen still folded her stomach and caused her whole body to feel the nausea.

"If you stay where I ask you to, you will never need to consider a moment of it." He could see her pale complexion as the flashbacks started. He hid the gutting pain it caused him.

"I cannot see the goodness of murder." She replied softly between sobs.

"For it is not your right, it is a God's." Cernunnos, shaking his head once again, struggled to make eye contact with his love, for the anguish her distress was causing him was unlike any scars of war.

"Is there not a moment of you that considers this terrible?" She stared, blankly into open space.

"Yes, there is. But the filthy actions of so many humans, hell bent on generating evil, have left me with no options." Cernunnos explained.

"You must be deviant of spirit to muster the callousness to do it." Kenina snarled. He immediately responded.

"Is that what your heart tells you? My darling, your perspective is only built to blame me. Do you not see that it is not the Machiavel who is deviant, in his clear reality? Rather it is the one who falls madly in love with him, ignoring her own dark usage of an ambiguous morality. Pursuing him without understanding the depths of his nature or how it mirrors her own?"

Kenina paused reluctantly and processed his words. There remained one important question to override them all.

"Can you bring peace to the cities of Alba by doing this?" She asked without inflection in her tone.

"It is fully possible. If the humans heed this as their fair warning. I come first, my father comes second. The Great God's mercy is far more deeply steeped in cynicism. The fishes flow first, and the sharks of judgement follow after." Cernunnos was direct and certain.

He then pulled the bear rugs away from Kenina who was still cold. Something obvious from her chattering teeth. "My love, will you bestow on me the trust to warm you in my arms? How can I show you the care I have for you?" His voice returned to the gentle tones that she had become familiar with as he removed his long coat. Kenina simply nodded and allowed him to pull her in towards him and replace the rug over them both. Kenina still had a few tears to shed and they trickled down his chest. Pulling his heart with each new droplet. Under the pillow, assumedly placed there some time before, were cloths that had been dipped in herbal antiseptics. Cernunnos carefully removed Kenina's blouse, which although she had not yet seen the cloths, was not difficult. She fought not amidst her exhaustion and weakened muscles. Cernunnos was lost in Kenina's fire shaded eyes as he began dabbing one of the cloths across the slashes in her skin. The cloth was cooling to Kenina's injuries and her troubled heart. She began to breathe more evenly and even sigh in relief as the slashes in the most vulnerable places he would tend to whilst pressing his lips against her forehead delicately, reaffirming his intimate bond to her. His other arm lay under her neck and wrapped around her back to stabilise her in safety.

CHAPTER 12:

Wolves of Warning

Dawn broke with the whistles and rustles of birds. Their melodious chaos was welcome that morning. Snow covered the land of Alba and not a moment of it had missed out. Robins framed the scenery and deer sprung as if they weighed not a thing. Kenina was first to awake and the birds lured her into the snow. She began throwing berries to them as it would be difficult to forage in the white fallen clouds. Kenina then noticed a very familiar sound of wolves. Remembering suddenly that they matched the howls of the wolves who would dine outside of her hut in Emrun city. She loved them for they had given her many a warning over the years. The wolves began to surround her and Kenina danced as they circled. She threw the last of the berries into the air and she sat with the wolves. She began to tell them stories of her adventures since she had last known them. Home felt for a flittering moment as if it was once again in reality. Among the wolves she felt she could hear the ancient songs her mother once serenaded.

Cernunnos became curious after waking to the sounds and crouched down by the shelter entrance, watching Kenina and the wolves. He was impressed with her connection to nature, which he never allowed himself time to discover before. Kenina then became uneasy and knew that something was very wrong.

"My love?" Kenina called out without making her tone harsh. In an instant Cernunnos flew to her side.

"I am with you. What do you fear?" He quizzed.

Kenina turned to look at him and suddenly took action.

"My love, you must take the meats in our shelter and you must throw them into the rushing stream below the valley. The water there is strong enough that it will carry the meats far away from here. Let the wolves chase after the lot." She quickly unleashed her plan without explanation. Knowing that this was his time to show her his trust, Cernunnos pulled all of the deer carcasses that they had left into his arms, took them across the valley and let them be dragged by the stream. His mind was confused. How could Kenina discover danger before him? Nonetheless he threw every piece of meat into the stream and the wolves began soaring after them. Cernunnos was glad that the stream was not frozen over.

Cernunnos strode back with definition. Ready to put Kenina's mind at ease. He had not sensed any danger and intended to calm her nerves. But upon his return, Kenina was nowhere within sight. He also began feeling a strange and cryptic unease. Cernunnos pulled armour onto his body and left the shelter again, carrying a single heavy sword. As he walked along the pathway in the direction of Kenina's old shelter, he heard a whisper.

"Hey!" Cernunnos shot his eyes to the sound and looked up to see his love high in a pine tree. She beckoned him to join her frantically.

Cernunnos climbed with such ease as if to fly.

"What do you see Kenina?" Cernunnos whispered.

"These wolves have warned me of danger for many years and I don't believe they came to me for pleasantries." Kenina began.

Cernunnos suddenly clasped his hand over her mouth and hid her under his coat. She didn't struggle.

Two men of hair like hers came striding along the path below, with red belts. They were warriors with grim faces covered in battle scars. They were openly conversing.

"In this forest is Kenina of Emrun. Somewhere she hides. But she is the sister of the Great Brothers of Emrun!" Came one of the men's words. His speech loud and brash. Cernunnos' eyes narrowed and an unshackled anger began to heat up. The devilish man continued unaware.

"You can find her by following the wolves ahead. They love her dearly and the foolish beasts will give her away." His words now on point with Kenina's fear. Cernunnos drew Kenina closer to his body with one arm and a raw masculine rage concentrated his blood. The man below still continued, "I am telling you what the witches have said. If a warrior can capture her, her brothers will be raised back to life at the very moment she is sacrificed before the city." His voice was one that only the bloodthirsty would herald proudly. Kenina gasped deeply in panic. The men heard her and began to scan the area slowly, grinning horribly. She began considering how she could trick them into destruction. But Cernunnos looked at her with a majestic definition that she had never seen before.

Although there were two men, Cernunnnos slowly raised his sword bearing arm above him. His grip of Kenina tightened as he built up force within to strike. Waiting for the men to align as he wished below them. At that second, in one divine swipe, Cernunnos plummeted his sword out of the tree, putting a herculean, tight spin on it. Cernunnos roared with unbridled emotion as he let go of the sword. The sheer force he exerted on the spin and the sharpness of his weapon decimated both men at once. There was an audible growl coming from Cernunnos' lungs even for a minute after. Kenina grabbed Cernunnos' body and wept at the sight and the terror of what had almost befallen her. Brightest blood of orange and red stained the crisp snow. She could not lift her face from his chest.

Cernunnos cast a spell of blessing to find the friendly wolves that had come to afford Kenina her survival and he held her tightly, gently dabbing kisses on her head.

"I am sorry that you had to witness such brutality my love. I shall cover your eyes, for it is all I can do." Cernunnos comforted.

Kenina suddenly looked up at him and pulled his coat.

"I am crying because I recognised them. The men you spared on the battlefield, for a digression in pursuit of me. Do men on both sides really wish me dead?" Kenina looked to him for an answer. Cernunnos sighed before responding.

"Morrigan has allowed the rumour that you are here in the forest, to spread so that we might find the bloodthirsty among the men of Alba. The battle you witnessed was started because a man claimed to have captured you and the two cities fought over who should earn the right to sacrifice you. It is good that I saw you atop the cliff for otherwise a great evil would have pursued you instead." He was breathing heavily with frustration at the pain he could not guard Kenina from. "This is why I insist that you remain in my shelter when you are alone, or when I tell you to. A great magic wards my hut and you will never be found." He said this as he picked Kenina up and swiftly descended the tree. "Be aware Lady of My Heart, your good kindness towards nature has found you favour with the Great God of Alba for a great many years. You have even settled my doubts. You will not be the fodder of those in line for terminal judgement."

Kenina bowed her head slightly with gratefulness and then replied. "Thank you for sparing me, God of Alba. I am sorry that I saw in you a great darkness when you were in fact drawing blood on my behalf, that it never stain my name or cause my own blood to seep onto the icy glens. I now see your great loyalty and sacrifices." This brought peace and duty to Cernunnos' heart as he listened and watched over her, delighting internally at the development of her character day by day. He knew she was finally resting true trust upon his shoulders.

"It is easy to misconstrue the acts of a good man for acts of darkness when he battles darkness forcefully. But only when you have never truly known the light. Your life has come to birth in darkness, and although the new glimmers of light are painful, I encourage you to stay with me and I will lead you to your victory."

Cernunnos spoke with a wise air. Kenina found it wonderful to begin listening to him carefully and see goodness come to fruition despite the means required to acquire it.

She had but one more question.

"Your violence is always placed in a direction to battle for good. What will happen if you turn your face to another dark morality? Is it safe, to lack an innocent niceness? Or are you to settle with merely being unpredictably complex?" She looked serious as if to figure him out.

"I would more naturally prefer to be nice. But nice men don't save worlds. Heroes handle their rich complexity in the same way a skilled hunter spins and aims his spear. All in the undying pursuit of the greater good. But without great skill, self-control and purpose, a complex man's actions become nothing more than a dangerous chaos of intention and unsynchronised blathering, soon to wane and retire to be hated. I don't pray to be nice, I pray to be skilled at discerning the moments to raise my sword."

CHAPTER 13:

Kenina's Power

As with all of their returns, the hut of Great Magic was a joyous sight and it brought peace. Cernunnos took initiative to take Kenina's hand and walk with her, matching their strides in harmony. Yet, something else was going through her head. The sheer ground tremoring power he heralded and had just revealed, did something most strange to her emotions. Suddenly craving him deeply. The chance to have power was surprisingly righteous to both of them, but she wasn't ever going to let go now. Kenina knew in her heart that to keep him, she would now have to reveal the capability she concealed in the body of an innocent damsel. Arousal was of many things in the world. Fear, anger, love. But in any form, it is most long lasting when two souls lock their powers.

Drawing each other in with the bloody-minded possession to remain stuck. Cernunnos knew not what was building and had a whimsical air, but he was about to be a desperately grateful god. He was about to praise her delectable attitude that would bring him now onto his knees.

Cernunnos guided Kenina into the hut and once inside, he removed Kenina's coat and boots and began patting the snow from them. Kenina now had eyes of definition. A distinguished determination. She stepped over to him as he continued and slid his own coat from his shoulders. Her touch was always soft and gracious. She patted the snow from his coat and laid it beside his weaponry. Quickly, she returned to his side to remove his boots. Then returned again and delicately ran her fingers across his shirt before very softly pulling his shirt off before running her nails across his back in smooth swirling patterns. This caused him to pause from patting her coat for a moment. He carried surprise on his face, for there was conviction to Kenina's actions. A colour of her character he had not been aware of. A colour that had been expertly concealed.

Kenina closed her eyes to the music of his deep, relaxed exhalations that were a result of her influence on him. A mighty god kneeling before her, increasingly intoxicated by her slightest touch, made her feel the great force of feminine sensuality. This power connected immediately to her as if to have been summoned. But instead of being summoned from somewhere else, it began to roar and catch alight from inside Kenina's own soul. As the flame grew, she began to tip her own head back and sound her overwhelm almost voicelessly. Cernunnos instantly felt her call and locked it into his heart. He could never miss her wordless imploring, no matter how hushed. At once, Cernunnos stood tall and cascaded the boots, coats and sword to the corner of the hut in one forceful swipe, before once more drawing his unbridled attention to his love.

Kenina turned away and glided across the hut, her hair following a little lifted. She slid into the bed with a doe's eyes and smiled with a serene sweetness. It was clear now, Cernunnos was not the only one who had a holy charm. Kenina heralded her femininity as a hypnotic beacon to her god and Cernunnos was now willingly captivated. He strode to her side of the bed and pulled back the bear fur rugs with puissance, for a second taking in the sight of Kenina before him. As he looked, he realised that she was in fact wearing his shirt and not her own. It was impossible to tell when she had done this, or why he hadn't noticed. But almost as if she somehow had a new familiar smell, now adorning his clothes, Cernunnos took her hand nearest to him and clasped it tenderly. After a moment, being lost in her eyes, he kissed her fingers and held them there against his lips. Just to breathe in her perfume of warm fires and frosted pines. Kenina looked at Cernunnos' eyes which seemed in their swirling colours to contain every element. Somehow she took a journey every time she gazed into them.

There stood before them, was an all encompassing love for the dark and light within their hearts. Without conditions to alter. This love had surpassed judgement gradually, as each day passed. The decision to give up an inherent doubt for others and proceed wholeheartedly and unblinkingly into a world of unknown emotion, was a feat of great courage for both souls facing one another. With no armour, no wolves, no swords and no illusions. Both souls had their chance to finally give and receive without refrain or fear. Their crux, a mutual fear of deceit and their deadlock of morals, left them in a place where empathy could fly out of them and flutter to the other. Butterflies oh so delicate that had before been quashed in pursuit of safety and security. Power became a combined effort and cleverness became an act of two minds.

Cernunnos at last, lay himself atop of Kenina. He drew the bear fur blankets over them both and he began to assertively remind her of the seductive and utterly provocative charms he had. Kissing and nuzzling her neck, he unveiled her of his shirt with his hands. She also pulled his remaining clothes out of her way. There was only one direction in mind. Two focussed souls, hell bent on filling each other's thoughts abundantly. One far stronger, one devastatingly enticing. They felt unabridged in expression and did not hide a moment of their bodies from one another. Their desires, honestly and vulnerably, were expressed with every breath and sound. Outside, the fire pit erupted and broke free of kindling. There wasn't a glowing ember caged. A dance and a drum. Flames soared high and turned the night sky red, orange and sienna. The night remained ablaze and unfettered amidst sharp snow and ice. Impossible to dampen.

Morning came to, from its dizzy night exhausted. Cernunnos and Kenina saw no reason to leave the hut. Thus, they began to relax totally and completely in the knowledge that they were together and rejoined. Snowy breezes eventually seeped through the material of the hut curtains and brought a welcome breeze to their heated bodies.

Cernunnos reached over Kenina to pull out a small box behind the bed. A stained, ancient oak box. With a smile, he handed it to Kenina and she opened it.
His eyes waited for a response as she figured it's access. As the box opened, the smell of ancient beauty emanated and Kenina couldn't help but breathe it in. There inside, lay a necklace of Celtic knots made from the finest light metal. Kenina seemed unsure what to do with it. It looked as if to be a possession of a monarch.
"Let me place it around your neck Kenina." Cernunnos began to slide it away from the box. "This is my mother's, but she insisted that one day I should share it with someone I love, so that she might eternally show them mercy." Once Cernunnos had fastened the jewellery to Kenina's neck, it sat beautifully. He beamed with generous pride at his love's grace and enchanting looks. Now stunningly framed. "She will one day love to see you

wear it." Cernunnos leant in towards Kenina as he said this. Kenina inhaled smoothly and without labour, for peace overcame the mind. She then placed her hand on the necklace, running her fingers along the smooth metal.
"Yes, I sincerely hope that she does." Came the sweet reply.

For many days after that, the couple lived in bliss. Taking time to speak with one another and understand each other's passions. Hunting was easier together and the increasingly frozen nights were akin to summer for them. Despite the separation from all the other people in Alba, Kenina did not mind. Seemingly, Cernunnos did not think about his distance from the Heavenly Realms either. One evening, sat in front of the dancing flames of the pit, Kenina asked Cernunnos why he had been so terrible towards her but never caused her harm. Wanting reassurance that she was in fact a woman of goodness in his eyes. Cernunnos finally opened to tell the tale.

"Kenina, the works of the Heavenly Realms are steeped in confusion for mortals during their life here, but you and your terrible brothers have a heritage in the Heavenly Realms." As he spoke Kenina looked up in surprise. "Your father was a god. He was brutal by nature and he waged many impossible wars before my father banished him to Earth to handle his character. He married your mother, who knew his capacity, but she gave him children in hope that the godly line would now have a gentler spirit ruling it. She had the gentlest and most sacrificial spirit of all the women of Emrun. Her first three sons brought nothing but anguish, but the Great God looked down from above and saw you differently. Your mother wished she could one day tell you about your father. But my father insisted that you should not know in childhood. Your father was destroyed by Morrigan shortly after your birth, to prevent his return to the Heavenly Realm after waging even greater wars on Earth. It seemed to be a mighty burden for a soul so young as you were. Once you became an adult, your mother didn't want to cause you trouble." He explained and then swallowed before continuing to the worst scene in his mind.

"One day, my mother visited the land of Alba to bring the spring. Forgetting that your brother's heavenly ancestry would allow them to see her. Dain, snuck along behind her. Suddenly, in a blind fit of ancestral rage, as his father's hellish spirit cast upon the wind, Dain slashed my mother's back with his sword. I was not far from them and managed to pull her away. But upon returning her to the Heavenly Realm, I wished to take a final bloodied revenge on all descendants of the Devil of Fire." He paused as Kenina's face fell pale. But decided to go on regardless. "As I left, my father warned me that you may still have a good heart and I should spare you. I told him that I wanted to destroy all of the city, but not your mother. Partly because she was a good woman and also because of the pain I felt seeing my own mother suffer. My father then sent my cousin Morrigan to light a fire over Emrun and give your mother the choice to stay with you in this life, or follow her sons into death and attempt to bring salvation to their souls before my father. Besides, whoever Morrigan should slaughter wrongfully will immediately have an audience before my father in the Heavenly Realm and they may argue their case. Your mother chose to follow her sons, but sent you to the forest because I am quite certain she knew I would be here. I don't know how she knew exactly, but I was reluctant to take responsibility for you. Even though it was according to her final wish and my father's warning. After all, they were considering raising you up to the Heavenly Realms in the place of your father. But I couldn't imagine a descendant of him, ruling the worlds with kindness. You, my dear, have changed my mind in its entirety." Cernunnos spoke matter of factly without consideration for Kenina's shock as he finished opening up her history.

"I'm a goddess?" She responded.

"You will be after your life on Earth is finished. That is the reason you can see me and this hut. It is the reason you can rest in my arms." He replied. "But for now you must focus on your good character." When he finished his sentence, Kenina looked out across the Glens with a slight glaze upon her eyes. Cernunnos picked her up, placed her inside the hut and pulled the curtain across so that it became darker inside and also warmer. "Do not fret for now. We shall simply get you through this life Little Fire. The life to come next will not be simple or easy. Or even unending. I will even have to return there soon, but not for a while. My father will become old in his destiny before assuming a new one. I shall take his place in time."

Kenina sat up in the bed, zoning in and out of her personal thoughts. Cernunnos waited patiently for her next question.

"What does that mean for me? I have to live in a world where entire cities want to sacrifice me? Alone? Are you going before me?" Cernunnos pulled her into his arms and lullabyed his response.

"Kenina my dearest one, let us not think of that. I shall bargain with my father and do for you what I can even from the Heavens. After all, it is best that you live your life here first. We are so in love, that opposing realms will see you as my greatest weakness. Let us keep the peace of you being hidden here. Besides, it will be a long time before I must return." These words calmed Kenina and she put off the emotion of him leaving her one day and they huddled into the blankets to sleep soundly. Him, caressing her every once in a while to reassure her spirit.

CHAPTER 14:

Separate Souls

Morning came bitterly and it was still. Not a breeze blew, not a snowflake fell. It had crept over rivers and streams. It had rested upon the edges of the hut. Birds did not serenade, nor did any take to the sky. Wolves fell to dormancy and deer did not chase winter ruts. Air was drying to inhale and Kenina began to cough, which awoke her.

Looking to her side, Cernunnos was not beside Kenina. Clattering sounds penetrated her ears and sharp metals clashed, cutting through icy silences. There were shouts of argument and Kenina swore that even the ground yelped at the calamity. Kenina sat up and tried to peer through the hut curtain from afar. Her eyes adjusted and she could now see a figure standing before a wintry position. There, covered in scars in the shelter entrance, was Cernunnos. He was glistening only from the tears he had been shedding. He threw rocks and bellowed into the frozen air. Clearly hysterical. Kenina remained where she was, for she knew not what had done this.

Kenina stared unblinking in shock and noticed many angels in armoury carrying their weapons to the sky. A sight she had not seen before. Crystal and white, their wings made no sound. All were gesturing angrily, but looked as if they might be spirits of heaven. One of the angels called out and melted ice in the air.

"You may defeat us, but you will not defeat Kingship! You have only moments left to recover your reputation. Be assured that we will not return, instead the one to come will deal with you as he wishes." The angel's voice was clear and not sinister. Instead, he presented the warning with a look of solemnity. Cernunnos screamed at the sky and threw his sword to the ground. Tears melted images into the frost below. Images of separation and lone fires. Another darker image was forming and Cernunnos trod it into mud.

With no majesty adorned, Cernunnos walked to Kenina's bed side with a face dipped in dread.

"My father's guards appeared to return me to the Heavenly Realm upon his command." He breathed heavily. "I fought them all off me to speak to you, but I must go immediately to avoid disgrace to my father."

Kenina immediately sat up and yelled with an ear piercing pitch.

"How can you do this? What am I supposed to do? Where will I go? I have no life here! I know not a soul and I am at the murderous hands of Alba!" She threw more questions and he shook his head thinking of how to calm her.

"Kenina I have no choice. With his age he can't stand for me to be away." He knew his heart wrenching duty. "My combatting of his guards could even be construed for a war declaration. You must live your life here, there is no way to bring you with me." He stated.

"Do you not understand oh God of Escape? Every city has vowed to destroy me!" Kenina couldn't hide the panic.

"Please my love, understand. My father would not call me back unless there was a danger to the Realms in my absence." Cernunnos knew this wasn't comforting, but was devoid of the words to repair.

"Then I will take my own life to join you." Kenina announced and almost choked as the words escaped. Cernunnos reacted instantly, stretching his hands towards her.

"No! Kenina that will not allow you to reach the Heavenly Realms, but instead force you to repeat another life. Please, live your life. Please, my love, I will watch over you." Cernunnos was already moving away as bugle sounds came from the skies. He pulled on his boots and coat and looked at her in hopeless distress as he began his mighty ascension. His face, a result of her eyes. He felt in his soul that she would not continue this life's destiny.

So quickly and so mercilessly, Kenina saw that the

rest of her life would somehow have to continue without her love. Hoping it wasn't true, Kenina rubbed her eyes and paced around the shelter. She picked up his old shirt which lay on the floor and clung to the smell. His swords lay in the corner as if to be dogs missing their master. Such emptiness befell the woman who could visit no one, and take peace from nowhere. Her first action was to throw some deer meats Cernunnos had left her, outside of the hut. Hoping to lure her canine guards into keeping watch. But she knew they would not visit until nightfall and more deadly soldiers could be following them.

Meanwhile, Cernunnos was finally approaching the Heavenly Realms looking beaten and angered. His father was awaiting him at the gates of the All Worlds Palace. A place people only knew in dreams of gold, but to Cernunnos it was home. The architecture stood proud, but the Great God's son stood limp. Staring blankly at the ground. The walls were tall, while this son of the Great God looked small.

"Cernunnos my son, lift your stance. You accomplished what you left to do, didn't you?" The Great God questioned, aware of Cernunnos' weak disposition.

"Yes father. Morrigan remains still to finish her work over the city of Emrun. I spared the youngest daughter of Fire." Cernunnos replied monotonously and still focussed to the ground.

"Your sparing of the young girl shows a great wisdom within you. Not every kin of evil raises themselves by the same path. Sometimes the pain it causes them generates a repelling as if South to South and North to North." He noticed that his son was more damaged of spirit than body. "Do you not agree?" He asked.

Cernunnos looked up at his father in brokenness, unable to process the gaping hole his heart possessed.

"I agree wholeheartedly." Came his sullen reply. Remembering the way he had treated Kenina in the beginning. Regretting every moment of coldness now.

The Great God allowed his son to retire to his chamber to wash and adorn his royal garments.

It had been a long time, but Cernunnos was comforted to at last be back home with his familiar friends, family and belongings. For a little while after getting dressed, Cernunnos sat on the end of his bed and wept into the towel he had used to dry his hair. His mind flashed to Kenina's words suggesting that she might end her life and he hoped dearly that she wouldn't choose to do that in order to be given another life with a different destiny. After all, the tribulations of the life she was living were immense. His arms tightened as he sobbed. Weeping in a way he had never done before. Knowing that the love he vowed to guard, was now alone in a world of murderers without him.

In the enchanting forests of Alba, Kenina had been

subsisting for a number of days now. Her fire never lit, but she found ways to keep old berries and plants frozen under the Earth in defense of hunger. There wasn't a vision to smile at, nor a future notion of joy. Kenina started to notice the black Shuck sometimes distant. In the corner of her eye his ratten fur swept past. Occasionally his eyes pierced red across the forest. At first he was distant, never inviting. Each night brought him closer. One can't fight that which does not attack. She merely assumed that he had taken pity on her. But an omen is clear in the spirit's discernment. His howl was chilling, but somehow boiled her blood and shivered her spine.

The shelter still provided safety if Kenina heard footsteps of warriors. They came along more frequently now. The pain Kenina had felt across the months of loss, left a numbness that was indistinguishable from the effects of winter. Nights were long and days were partial. Stars were covered by snow clouds and starving animals turned on Kenina in starvation. Bears, foxes, wolves. All were a battle of their own. But Kenina continued to survive. The reason to keep fighting appeared more and more to be a superfluous one as each confrontation commenced.

More time passed and Kenina sat in a tree to survey the forest in search of a possible meal. From her high point she caught the sight of stag horns. At first thinking nothing of it, they looked familiar. Kenina's heart overflowed with joy. These antlers were pacing into the distance and Kenina dropped down onto the forest floor in pursuit. Through brush and through bracken. Through fern and through ivy, Kenina tried to catch up. The antlers continued into a clearing in the glen. Kenina stopped and watched, feeling tired and unable to catch up. She breathed in to shout to him, as these antlers entered the clearing in entirety. There stood, a stag. It looked at Kenina nervously before bouncing into a distant wood.

Kenina's heart dropped to the floor before her legs did. Would she live this life forever? It became clear that she could not go on waiting for her love. He was simply never coming back for her. She couldn't chase deer into the woods in hope of the supernatural. With a sigh, Kenina got up and realised that her destiny was now in hand. Perhaps in another destiny they might meet. Although not likely, Kenina's tears would flow regardless. The time to end misery would come when the next full moon arrived. Marking three months since the destruction of Emrun. Kenina rested her body on the forest floor, and thought about how she should prepare to await the day. Fresh flowers in the mess of brush were almost soporific. In the middle of noon's daylight, Kenina saw darkness befall her eyes.

The Heavenly Realms lived on regardless of the withering love. A maid knocked on Cernunnos' chamber door and asked him to join his family at dinner. She noticed his swollen eyes and quickly ran a cloth under cold water, offering it to him to hide the swelling. Cernunnos was happy to see her again, as she had been his maid for more than a hundred years and had seen him grow up in time.

"Young one, I have never seen such depth of emotion inside of you before. Whatever befell you on Earth has made you much wiser in simply a month. But do grasp the wisdom to keep moving forwards. After all, your father's duties will soon be yours in his old age and you must decide the fates of the peoples of Alba." She rested her hand on his arm as she spoke. "Young one, emotion grows slowly for some, but once it arrives it is no less intense." She added this thought before leaving his room to continue her duties. Cernunnos followed on to the dining room.

At the table, his family called to him. His mother, cousins and others were there to welcome him back to the Heavenly Realm. Cernunnos was filled with love, but still a chasm opened where Kenina once stood. He swallowed and feigned a smile, knowing somehow he would have to move on. In case Kenina chose another way or found another love on Earth. His family ate with him and chatted, which was a welcome distraction. Then his mother stood up and walked to the kitchen door to call a maid to fetch some more wine. With her back to Cernunnos he could see a slash still present across her back covered only lightly by a strap line dress. He shuddered and thought of the Brothers of Fire. He shook his knee nervously to think of a way to explain his love for their kin. Not that it mattered anymore.

As evening brought crickets and owls, Cernunnos sat outside on an old bench at the side of the palace. The floral grounds framed by trees, were kissing the day's bees goodbye and Cernunnos watched in stillness. As the evening began to bear its perfume, a cousin of his appeared and sat beside him. Cuinn. A man of great wisdom, but someone Cernunnos didn't have the privilege of seeing often. Cuinn was not a warrior. Nor was he so mighty in stature. He wore only plain palace clothes of white and did not leave the Heavenly Realms very often. Instead, even the greatest of soldiers came to him for reassurance. His mind was unmatched across all the realms. But as a result, Cuinn gave his time sparingly to others, knowing that his ability was addictive, especially for the lost.

"So, how are the old antlers faring?" Cuinn joked, pushing his friendly hand into Cernunnos' shoulder. "Oh god, you know I've left them on Earth!" Cernunnos suddenly realised and broke into a slight laugh.

His cousin wittily replied, "oh my! Something must have distracted you!" But he lost his jesting expression as Cernunnos looked at the ground and swallowed hard to avoid tears.

"Cernunnos. Pray tell, what is the matter?" Cuinn asked before sensing the air's sorrow. "My gosh, have you fallen in love?" His cousin was never short of discernment.

"Madly, crazily. Stupidly." Cernunnos shook his head. Cuinn decided to impart his insights.

"My dear cousin, do you know that in life, when something is right, you have to battle for it? For losing it will always be most painful. Your duty is to the Heavenly Realm in this instance. But why don't you wait and see what she does? Perhaps she shall surprise you." He looked into the distance and placed his hand back on Cernunnos' shoulder, to reassure him and also to detect more of his situation. "Time may not heal, but it does reveal every unknown." Came his final offering of knowledge.

Cernunnos nodded and stood up. "I'm sorry my cousin, I must retire to my chamber to be alone." He stated in monotone.

Cuinn did not argue, he simply tilted his head to him and then sat back in his chair to gaze upon the fresh night's stars. A sure look of sage presented on his face just as it did his words. Two very different characters indeed, but Cuinn's dark hair and eyes could have been tied to his cousin since birth.

CHAPTER 15:

The Work of Wisdom

As time went on, Cernunnos began to adjust to the loss of his love. Developing a routine and slowly becoming jovial again. He attended meetings with his father and was showing his prowess as the future ruler. The Great God was proud of Cernunnos' works but decided to test him further. Cernunnos' tactical capacity was incredible, but could his generosity be trusted?

"Cernunnos I fear I may have made a mistake." His voice sounded with command. Cernunnos immediately lifted his head to reply, "father, what is it that has come to pass?"

"My son, I fear I have given you a warrior's spirit but not encouraged a hint of mercy and compassion. Tell me, if you can prove to me your goodness?" He spoke with an air of challenge.

"My father, I may not know the courage behind generosity in its fullness, but I have met those who have and I admire them. I hope that my actions to protect the good people of Alba will shine in clarity. But I can only do this if you allow me to act." Cernunnos'

reply was simple but filled with awareness.
"You wish me to find a way for you to prove your love for all good people of Alba? Very well. Give me some time." Came his father's response.

Cernunnos got up from the meeting table once his father had stepped away. But he felt uneasy as his mother walked in and called him to the gardens. She had a look that anyone would recognise in someone who had something to say, but couldn't establish how best to portray it, in hope of a positive response. Cernunnos strode behind her through the palace. She was so graceful, one could be mistaken and say that she was in fact flying. Cernunnos followed her, past ornate paintings of Great God's before his father. Through the old corridors of his childhood. Eventually, she stepped out into the floral garden, now alive and bright with the day's animals.

As they surveyed the estate, his mother began to explain her intentions.

"My son, it is time that you marry someone here in the Heavenly Realm. Your father and I have ascertained that there is a lady here. She is the only woman we consider suitable for you. I wish for you to meet her later today."

"A lady here in the Heavenly Realms?" Cernunnos exhaled with anguish and disappointment.

"We know that you may be unsure about the union perhaps, but a prophecy was foretold about your soulmate and she has fulfilled it." She saw his dejected expression but continued, "it may not suit you now, but it will mean great things for the future of our realm." Cernunnos could not argue with her for he loved her dearly and wished never to cause his mother to feel sadness after nearly losing her on that fateful spring morning. With a reluctant breath he agreed to meet the woman. "Please go and report to your father now and he will see you before you meet her." She finished before gliding into the distance to assess some flowering roses. Another woman joined her in the distance, but Cernunnos couldn't work out who it was. Assumedly a new gardener.

In Alba, things were worse. The ground was lighter, and the air heavier. There was a soul missing. Kenina did not have the heart to remain in this life of hers. As a new sun rose after the full moon, a silence crystallised in the morning frost. The night before had been fateful. Upon seeing the moon, Kenina had walked along the old path to her first shelter. It was so small and the fire pit had been so trodden that it couldn't even warn her. In a single continuation of motivation, Kenina eventually arrived at the forest edge. There lay the two warriors she had tricked. A terrible smell emanated and her body couldn't stand it, Kenina nonetheless pulled the full armoury from one of the men. His body was almost completely returned to dust. She wished for the same fate. Kenina heaved the armoury, from chain mail to helmet, onto her weakened body. A sword, she also took from the corpse. She was thin from the winter's lack of provision and nothing could fit her. Kenina didn't care. The helmet covered her gaunt, grey face from recognition.

Then the journey began to Emrun city. Kenina hurried with what capacity she had past the boulder upon which Kallan's apparition had appeared many days ago. Wishing not to be stopped or prevented. She stumbled down the hill towards the central point of Emrun. Nothing stood and ashes caught in the wind. Kenina coughed and stumbled over the open crematorium she once called home. Memories of her mother Lilith returned and her sword bearing hand now shook uncontrollably. Tears fell and she gave them no time to settle anywhere. As she continued her pursuit, three ravens flew overhead and began to sound their hell raising screeches. Kenina ignored them and ran forwards to where a shadow loomed ahead and Kenina gritted her teeth. Whoever the shadow was, Kenina was sure of their name. The shadow faced away from Kenina, a hood covering their head as they scanned Emrun from East to West. Kenina raised her shield away from her and screamed an unholy cry to the night sky as the full moon rose. She ran straight towards the shadow who swung around above the ground, reacting to the noise. They raised their own sword and slashed Kenina's throat in the same way they had decimated her city.

East to West.

Kenina immediately began to choke and her already limp body collapsed to the ground. Laying in the ashes, Kenina attempted a gargling breath or two, seeping away from her beloved Alba. As the deadly shadow watched, the soul of Fire visibly faded into a memory. Eyes closing and body no longer grasping onto life, blood stained the glen grass under her. Frost began to melt around her and smoke poured from the ground. The shadow was confused by this and pulled the helmet from Kenina's head roughly. Red hair and a young woman's face fell out. Far from a bloodthirsty warrior. In sudden shock, the shadow shouted, cracking the ground beneath.
"KENINA!!"

CHAPTER 16:

Deadly Destiny

Leaving the floral garden, Cernunnos returned to the palace and found his father in the throne room, sitting upon a throne of red silk and gold frame. One that had stood for many generations before him. He looked stern.

"My son, you returned from Earth with a frown and not joy. I do not know what happened to you there, nor shall I ask you to tell me. You have not chosen to and so I assume you do not wish to. But I have found for you a woman here in the Heavenly Realms who has fulfilled prophecy and will join you on the journey to your life's victory. Anyone you have met before will suffer into unimportance compared to the woman I have chosen for you. It will be perhaps your greatest challenge to love this person, but if you can love the girl I have here for you, I will be assured that you will love the people of Alba, even in darkness." The Great God had his chin down and his eyes struck Cernunnos' eyes with force.

"I shall never be truly happy with a woman other than the one I knew. But if the victory of Alba and my loyalty to it lies in the balance, I am prepared to make the sacrifice." His mouth became dry and bitter, but his eyes stayed with his father's to show his strength and preparedness.

"Then go to your bed chamber, where the lady awaits you. Do not be rude for I shall take this offense personally as being against my choices." His father finished his speech and sat back on his throne, looking majestically into the distance.

Cernunnos walked slowly to his bedroom and turned the handle to his door. He looked down as he entered, saying, "are you the one I must marry?"

"Yes, I am." The soft voice was familiar. Cernunnos looked up with a snap and met eyes with the lady. There in front of him stood a woman in the most beautiful white silken gown, with his mother's necklace clasped around her neck, covered slightly by her thick red hair.

"Kenina?" He asked, mouth agape. The lady continued to look down as she replied, "yes, my love." Cernunnos walked up to her and lifted her chin to look at him and quizzed, "how did you get here?" He looked deeply concerned and Kenina resisted his hand lifting her chin. Worry overtook Cernunnos and he inched her chin high enough to see her neck. His face was as flint as he saw what she was hiding. There was an almighty scar across her neck. Air fell out of Cernunnos' lungs. Kenina's tears sank into his fingers still holding her chin. Cernunnos' eyes followed suit. His face was still stern, feeling anger at the pain she had caused herself. But his eyes flowed with tears that refused to remain hidden. His voice whimpered before his love. "Kenina, what have you done?" He wiped her tears with his soaked hands. "What have you done to yourself? Did you want to escape me?" He dreaded the response to come as Kenina sniffed and wept.

"I have never felt so much pain as the morning you left my side. I stole the armoury from a warrior and covered my face in their helmet. I walked to the city of Emrun. Not recognising me, Morrigan took her sword to me. I remembered something you told me. Anyone that Morrigan killed undeservingly, would gain an audience with your father to make their case. Morrigan stood with me as I faced him, Declaring my love in a speech I thought was most hopeless." Her speech shocked Cernunnos but he had never felt such fulfilment or love. Cernunnos' cousin Cuinn appeared in the doorway.

"Cernunnos, the prophecy, do you not remember it? Your true love is to be half goddess, half woman. In pursuit of you, she would make the ultimate Earthly sacrifice to take the burden of royalty and become a goddess even before her time of responsibility had come. Here you stand before the greatest woman of your life! It was me that told your father to spare the woman who came looking for you, for I knew that the promised goddess was coming soon." Cuinn spoke with great joy and Cernunnos pulled Kenina into his arms, vowing unreservedly that he would be hers and she would be his. He would never allow another time or soul to separate them. Holding Kenina, he was shouting thanks to Cuinn. Cuinn smiled with his usual sage expression and then seemed to fade into the walls of the palace. Kenina began to weep with relief that she was finally again in Cernunnos' grasp, but she stifled her tears to express, "my dearest love, you said that my presence here would be a risk, for I am your greatest weakness. But I ask you in light of what I have just done to be by your side that you will have the courage to let me be your greatest strength for every day to come." She looked into his eyes and Cernunnos agreed without doubt. "Of course, my goddess." He sobbed in reply.

As they embraced, Kenina grew a little weak and slumped in Cernunnos' arms. Her head tipped low and the colours of her face ran dry. He began to panic but couldn't bring her back to him. Looking behind him, Cuinn was nowhere to be seen. Cernunnos shouted for his father and picked up Kenina in his arms. He took her lifeless body to the throne room before his father and cried out.
"Father! Father! Please! Help me!" Shouted the wailing god. He placed Kenina before his father's feet and begged him to bring her back to life. The Great God stood from his throne and approached Cernunnos, placing his hand upon Cernunnos' head. "My son, she is already waking up. Remember the trial this daughter has endured. Give her time to

rest and recover. When she fully awakes, you must carry her to your mother to inform them of your love formally. Do not make her walk and stand for a few days." He spoke without fear or haste and it calmed the soul of Cernunnos. "And, my son. When she has recovered, let her walk alone in the realms sometimes. Do not watch her every move, for now you must trust her capacity. If she needs you she will call, for the love she has is strong. You must now trust this goddess to honour you everywhere she treads."

The Great God vowed that Kenina would be given a new name and another story of her early life would be told to the people of Alba, to prevent retaliation against her marriage to Cernunnos. It was to be said from then on that her brothers were born of an evil spirit to separate them from the godly line, which now possessed a divine gentleness and compassion. Cernunnos agreed with this vow and tipped his head to look at his father, an innocent smile painted his face. The Great God could tell in the scent of rose blooms flowing from outside, that further dark trials would arise. But there were sacrifices that he was willing to commit to his ageing soul. These two innocent young royals needn't be burdened with such truths, in the spring of their life's destiny. The Great God's son still appeared as a boy in his fatherly glances. Memories danced. Laughter filled the room in his head. Yes, indeed, the Great God would say nothing of his knowledge and glide in majesty, to survey the realms from on high. Clouds shrouded his shoulders in awe.

As Kenina woke up on the floor of the throne room, Cernunnos lifted her and carried her to introduce her to his mother. The route felt shorter and excitement filled Cernunnos' heart as the feeling of Kenina in his arms brought a new life to his soul. As they reached the Palace gardens, Cernunnos stood still in pleasant surprise to see the woman standing with his mother admiring the rose blooms. The lady turned to look at the couple with eyes of the most gracious serenity. She smiled and spoke, "my daughter has always made the best decisions. I trust that you will never come to forget the almighty sacrifice she has made for you. Uphold your duty young son and be wed! Bring back victory to these lines!" Her words flew like liquid silver while she stood with the utmost poise in a flowing lavender dress. Mother Lilith.

Printed in Great Britain
by Amazon